Alsager Hay Hill

A Scholar's Day-Dream, Sonnets

And other Poems

Alsager Hay Hill

A Scholar's Day-Dream, Sonnets
And other Poems

ISBN/EAN: 9783337158521

Printed in Europe, USA, Canada, Australia, Japan

Cover: Foto ©Andreas Hilbeck / pixelio.de

More available books at **www.hansebooks.com**

A

SCHOLAR'S DAY-DREAM,

SONNETS,

AND OTHER POEMS.

BY

ALSAGER HAY HILL.

LONDON:

CHAPMAN AND HALL, 193, PICCADILLY.

1870.

TO MY MOTHER,

IN THE LIGHT OF WHOSE LOVE.

AND UNDER WHOSE DEVOTED CARE,

ALL THAT IS OF ANY WORTH,

EITHER IN MY LIFE OR WRITINGS,

HAS GROWN AND RIPENED,

I Dedicate these Pages.

PREFACE.

SOME of the poems in the present volume have already been published, and are now, by the kind permission of Mr. Charles Dickens, and other Editors of Magazines, reprinted here.

A few have had the good fortune to find their way into popular collections.

Many of the sonnets have also appeared at various times, and in various places.

Occupied of late years rather in the investigation of pauperism than the pursuit of literature, I am well aware that many of the poems here collected may be found wanting in that breadth, depth, and intensity, which only an entire devotion to poetry can develope. I have still, however, a hope that an old and abiding love of nature, coupled with some knowledge of the suffering masses (in whose interest many of these verses were written), may give to them a certain truth and earnestness, which larger opportunities of leisure might not have supplied.

ALSAGER HAY HILL.

NEW UNIVERSITY CLUB,
LONDON,
April, 1870.

CONTENTS.

Contents.

Contents.

A

SCHOLAR'S DAY-DREAM.

To the Memory of

H. S. H.

THE INSPIRATION OF WHOSE GOODNESS

LENDS TO ITS PAGES

ANY MERITS IT MAY POSSESS,

A SCHOLAR'S DAY-DREAM

Is Affectionately Inscribed.

A SCHOLAR'S DAY-DREAM;

BEING

AN EPISTLE IN VERSE WRITTEN FROM THE TEMPLE
TO A CURATE FRIEND IN THE COUNTRY.

HEN last, dear friend, we parted,
     months ago,
     Ere lavish Autumn strewed your roads
with gold,
Or pilgrim swallows gathered on the roof,
You bade me, when again I turned to town
And mingled in the busy crush of men,—
If any image of your pleasant fields
Or fragrant thought of quiet country ways

1

Should linger in the heart, and, o'er my books
Wafting the delicate breath of garden flowers,
Make the dull day seem lighter than its wont,—
To gather up some gracious memories
Of that sweet time that we had lived together,
And with what slender skill I might command
Weave fact or fancy into passing song.
Two months an idler free from task and rule,
And wandering at my will from place to place—
Now by the shores of gleaming Windermere,
And now far north afoot upon the moors—
Believe me when I found myself at home,
Once more within these studious Temple-bounds,
With grim old law-books staring from their shelves
That ill supply the place of leaf and flower,
Full often in the pauses of my toil
Rare glimpses of your village by the Trent
With all sweet sights and sounds that harbour
    there,
So steal upon my fancy unawares,

So take remembrance prisoner with delight.

That e'en as one in fabled fairy tale,

Led by the guiding spirit, wanders on

Through many a twinkling glade and forest-walk,

Deep in the trancèd realms of wonder-land :

So I, the while in witching thraldom bound,

High over street and tower am lifted up,

And, all-forgetful of the hour and place

That link me to the busier cares of life,

My heart is in your meadows far away,

My eye so full that it is dim with seeing,

My ear o'ercharged with music, and my hand

Warm with the answering grasp that speaks a friend.

For often falling hopeless in the heat,

And wearied with the ceaseless strain of care

That comes on one who vieweth day by day

Our mighty city, this vast sea of toil,

Yet knows not how to help,—thankful am I

That thou, dear friend, in many an hour of doubt,

When hand and brain were fainting in the strife,

Didst freely make me partner of thy joys,

And, gently leading forth the jaded soul

Away from all the tumult of the world

By dewy fields or murmurous river-side,

Didst offer me the benison of rest

And that sweet balm that is not born of fame,

Nor in the sleepless hurry of desire,

But settleth on the heart at ease and brings

New life for nobler work in after years.

All this, yea more, I owe to thee and thine :

So huge the debt I cannot hope to pay ;

Yet, while the spell is working in the brain

And airy memories gathered far and near

Are crowding all the chambers of my thought,

Well may I fix the vision ere it flies,

Hold back the forms that would be hurrying on,

And live for one brief hour that life again.

How dear to me are all your village ways :

For in the years gone by, a careless child,

I too have wandered in the woods and fields,

So happy that the dancing leaves o'erhead

Seemed but to wait the music of my thoughts

To answer every heart-beat; nest and flower,

The Spring's best first-fruits, every violet knot,

With all the peeping beauties of the hedge,

To me were treasure-trove of rarer worth

Than any I have gained in after times.

The song of thrush uplifted in the dawn

And wafted to my window on the breath

Of fresh-cut hay, that from the garden came,

With busier din of whetted scythe between;

The spangled starling running on the lawn;

The rabbit couched upon the dewy grass,

That knew he was a thief among the flowers

And pricked his fidget ears at every breath;—

All these are sights and sounds remembered well,

For every hour had some fresh bird or bloom

To mark it in the calendar of the heart;

Therefore I linger with a lover's spell
O'er every thought that yet can bring again,
From out the dusty store-house of the past,
Some token of that half-forgotten day :
Till all the recollections of my youth,
Warm with the kindling light of friendship, lie
Like April posies dropped upon a path
Where we had only looked for toil and din.

So fondly now I trace my steps once more
Through each familiar haunt that seems so old,
With every passing picture known and loved
Yet bringing still some freshness of delight ;
E'en as a letter read a hundred times
Is dear to him who knew the hand that wrote,
And now is cold for ever.   Yonder see,
In holy calm uprising on the sight,
The semblance of your quiet house of God,—
True heart of every village,—girt with graves
As simple as the simple folk below,

Yet all o'ergrown with random flower and moss

That weave their choicest pall above the poor,

And bribe to beauty every thought of death :

So tenderly the touch of Nature falls

That e'en her slenderest offerings at the tomb

Make fragrant all the threshold of the Spring.

There too, in shadow of the old lich-gate,

Beneath whose crumbling porch for ages past

The quiet pomp of village funerals

Has rested ere they gathered round the grave,

And earth's last rites were paid, three crosses
  stand,

Three tiny crosses, white as were the souls

Of those dear lambs that from a father's fold

The Master-Shepherd lifted to His own ;

And often when the early Spring is bright,

And the first violets twinkle through the grass,

Soft steps, that seem yet softer than the feet

Of the pert red-breast heralding their way,

Come to those crosses, and a sister's hand

Scatters a wealth of blossoms on the sod

That Death himself would wake for such a crown ;

While sometimes with her other little ones

Come pattering, and though they know not why

A lovely silence hallows all their ways,

E'en as the hush that falls upon the birds

Unwitting in the presence of eclipse.

There too a father brings a sterner grief,

And is not shamed to think his eyes are dry

And the hands empty, for his heart is strong

To make that grounded sorrow in the soul

True anchor of the years to come.   But here

I may not linger.   Let us follow now

Yonder green path that, through the clover-field,

Now humming as if every flower were bee,

Runs to the vicarage door.   Upon that lawn,

Still shaven for the purpose of our sport,

And where the straggling crow-foot dares not come,

How often have we sped the balls about,

How watched the rival creep from hoop to hoop,

So warily and with so still a hand
You'd almost deem his life was on the stroke
To miss or make it.   Even Walter there,
Fresh from the noisy realms of school-boy play,
And wild as any madcap in the din
And hurley-burley of the hockey-match,
Would watch as sagely silent as the hern
That waits the welcome ebbing of the tide,
Still as the stone he stands on.   Jessie too,
Her face as plump and beaming as the best
Of all the rosy apples that o'erhang
The gold-mossed garden-wall above the house,
Had many a curious doubt and grave appeal
About the right construction of the laws ;
Queen despot would she be of all the field,
A little Lady Solon on the lawn ;
But Jamie had a code she knew not whence,
And would not listen to her wise decrees ;
While, as for laws, he wanted but to win,
And cared not for the way : till, at the last,

The weight of age was thrown into the cause ;

And, wrangling still each mounted on a knee

Of that good grandsire known to both of us,

Yet better known to all the country flock

Whom he hath loved and led these thirty years.

Then, garrulous as twin swallows in the eaves

That answer each the other all the day,

They told the broken story of the game ;

How she had hit the ball into its place

And claimed her turn again ; but he, forsooth,

Said nay, and would not yield to anyone ;

He was for pushing onward to the goal,

And was not to be thwarted in his aim,

No, not by twenty.   So the battle went ;

And, in the ceaseless chatter of debate,

It seemed not easier to have played the judge,

And settled all the tickle points of strife,

Than, walking in the autumn-fields to part

Two reed-birds jangling in the osier-beds,

And bid them sing together. " Well, my chicks,"—

So ran the old man's judgment,—"both are right,

Both wrong; so take two kisses for your pains,

No damages to either side: and now

Suppose we three begin the game afresh."

This settled all. And many another bout

Can I remember on that croquet-ground,

When college friend or fellow-Templar came,

Free from the dust of chambers and of court,

To take a passing sip of village air

Ere plunging back into his sea of work;

And each had welcome. Who could doubt the hand

That grasped us on the threshold when we came?

(Our only title that we came with you.)

'Twas warm as though the pulses of his life

Had beat one tune with ours from boyhood up.

So kindly, too, the greeting on his face,

One almost thought, indeed, he was a friend

In some forgotten world that once was ours,

And yet again may waken at a touch,

Or word, or look, as often in the clouds,

Some wintry day, a tiny rift of blue,

Scarce bigger than the speedwell's glittering eye,

Brings back the shrouded Spring into the heart,

And fills the thought with flowers. His very voice,

As manly as the lips from which it came,

Had music in it never heard before,

Yet seeming part of memory the while

We listened. Every gleam upon his brow

Spake self-same message—welcome ! Such a man

Is nature's moulding, fashioned by the hand

That bids the oak uplift its valiant arms,

O'er-topping like a king the forest tribes

That gird his greatness : making dignity

No appanage of favour-doling State,

No surface-polish on the sculptor's work,

But part of being—woven to the strength

That shelters what is weaker, not o'erawes it.

A village pastor, be it even so,

Yet may he walk in quiet majesty,

Shepherd and king in one—without a crown,

But wearing all the royalty of love ;

Faith, hope, and kindness shining in his train ;

And followed by the countless tender deeds

That make the good man's glory while he lives,

And feed the lamp of memory after death.

A thousand blessings, breathed by one that knows

What friendship means, and knows that meaning
    more

From knowing him, are all that I can give.

Poor thanks, indeed, for such a noble gain,

Enriching all my after-growth of life ;

Yet haply better to his simple heart

Than other wealth which is not mine to give.

She too, the gentle partner at his side,

And constant as the shadow to the tree,

Glides with so soft a foot-fall on my dream

That utterance, in the light of such a face,

Sounds harsh as, in the moonlit summer eves,

To wake the sleeping silence of the woods

By word or whisper of our busy earth.

Yet can I not forego some tribute paid

To her that was the gracious ruling queen

Of all that home which thou hast shared so long :

Life running quietly beneath her sway,

As river to the single-shining moon

When all the stars are hid.   How tenderly

She took the trivial-seeming household tasks,

And made them, in the happy light of love,

Look beautiful as is an angel's work

Wrought silently before the mortal gaze

Of us that take, but know not whom to thank.

Among her children half a child for them,

And differing only as the full-blown flower

That crowns the early cluster from the bloom

That girds it.   Oh ! how fair a sight for us

Who live too much, or dream indeed we live,

In calmness high above all childish ways,

And think, perhaps, that in our books we find

A wisdom better than that early code

Which boyhood had engraven on the heart

Without the meted lessons of the schools;

Then rather learning most when least we knew

Our teacher: and 'twould seem that even now

Some letters of that finer-written creed,

Still underlying the strange palimpsest

Which we have scribbled in the name of art,

Will break upon us in the light of Spring,

Or flower, or child,—for these are but the same—

Wakening us to the life that used to be,

And is not dead within us, though we wrap

The cerements all so close about the heart

That some might deem the spirit could not stay

In such a swathing; happy are we then

Standing once more in sight of what we were,

And looking to the glories yet to be.

So guided to the inmost shrine by her,

Who playing with her children yet did yield

High homage truer than the sounding pomp

Of minster-choir, I have risen to be

More worthy of the joys I came to share,

And more believing in the sacred names

Of child and mother, dear indeed to me

As all the garnered memories of my youth

Can make them ; yet at times, too oft, I ween,

Amid the clamour of the world's highway

Whereon we fret and spend our little strength,

To be forgotten as some wild-flower's name

That needs to be respoken by a friend,

And then is fresh as on the summer-day

When first we plucked it.   Every childish freak

Or fancy guided by the gentle hand

Of such as she, though in itself but frail,

And passing with the fashion of the hour,

Is lovely to the trancèd after-thought ;

E'en as the slenderest bracken in the woods

Is lighted into glory when the moon

Falls on the forest, making every leaf

Dear as Endymion's lips.   Ah me ! to think

The days are gone when we could meet and feel

Her presence with us an abiding joy,

A saintly consolation in our grief,

A fount of beauty ever rising fresh

Beside the dusty paths of daily life !

And yet the grave, with all its cruel wrong,

Though it hath stolen the fairest flower of earth,

Robs not our memory of its cherished dower,

Nor sullies aught of that sweet worth which hath

No union with the perishing flesh and form

Which we called woman.   Even now there comes

A yet more blessèd presence to our souls

Than that fair shape which filled the outward eye

And made us think that heaven was nearer earth

Than in the times when we had known her not.

The seasons of delight that we have lived

Within the hallowed circle of her rule

Are dearer now than e'en they used to be.

As some home-landscape to the sailor's eye,

After long years returning, strikes more fair

Seen in the twilight, whence he conjures up

A thousand pictures of the days gone by,

Than in the flaming noon-tide of his youth,

When knowing all he wandered at his will,

And every tree was a familiar friend ;

So, shadowed into softer beauty, rise the hours

That we have lived together.

     Nor aught less

Do I recall those golden evenings spent

Beneath the bounteous shelter of that roof,

Where still she shone, our evening-star of mirth,

That seemed in every quarter of the sky,

And yet was ever centre ; passing bright,

Yet quiet in the zenith of its joy,

Though sometimes shadowed with a trace of grief,

Of grief gone by and lifted into trust ;

Yet making such a void within the heart

As only heaven shall fill. How blithely rang

The voices to the music in our glee,

Without a break, save when at intervals

Some babbler, like myself, that barely knows

Or sharp or flat, and never learned a note

Save what the woods could teach him, interwove

A random patch of talk between the tunes,

And made a grudged yet welcome breathing-space

And then the Vicar played his violin

As if his very heart-strings had been given

To make the tune go brisker—every one,

So catching seemed the trick of melody,

Had voice to sing, and gave it as the thrush

That on the first up-starting of the year,

While yet the wood is waiting for its choir,

Fills up the gleaming silence after showers.

You, too, had dainty measures all your own ;

And well, methinks, to such a warbled strain—

Half-mock, half-match of all the whistling tribe

That flood the summer woodlands with their notes

Mine ear could listen all the livelong night,

Till that I seemed o'ershadowed by the limes

Of Beaudesert, where in the hot July

The fly-catcher is chirping from the boughs,

Or seems, so light his fallings to and fro,

A-chase of his own shadow in the air ;

So wonderful the music that you made

To one, indeed, that only takes his key

From field and forest.   Then what store of song

Had he, our fellow-student by the Cam,

And now my brother-worker in the maze

So strangely passing by the name of Law !

What tuneful memories of the pleasant Rhine !

What airy German fancies caught in verse !

Rare treat for all.   One also of our choir,—

He, too, a brother toiler in the courts,

Yet taking from their heated tournaments

No stain of drought or dust about the heart,

But ever fresh with random rhyme and jest,—

Would break upon the moment with a catch,

Half-woven in the pauses of our mirth,

Half creature of the busy-working brain

That spun its gossamer fancies fast and wild

From every passing change, till each of us

Would find himself entangled in the mesh,

Our every feature glistening through the lines,

With just so much of satire in the song

As made us feel what little human gnats

At best we are, though to the generous sun

We spread our tiny wings, and think the day

Is richer for our stir.   His happy face

The while he jerked and jolted out the tune

Ran with so rare a ripple of delight,

And all his frame so mated with the mood,

You might have thought he would have slipped away

E'en as those wondrous shadows on the sheet

That take the eye of childhood, and are gone

Before we think to question whence they are.

So sped those treasured evenings till the time,

Thrice blessèd time, that hallows all the day,

When all the little household bent in prayer,

Master and servant, mother, child, and guest,

Close gathered in the room ; that more than church

Seemed for the while God's holiest shrine on
    earth;

His Spirit's resting-place—the heart of home.

Then he of whom I spake—our tender host,

And yet more tender father—in the midst,

With voice that seemed o'erburdened by its charge,

Half-tremulous, yet trustful in its quest,

Read from the Psalms of David, or the words

Of Him who, greater than all kings of earth,

Yet took the babes and blessed them on his knee :

And left the promise, " Wheresoever two

Or three are gathered in My name together,

There am I in the midst."   Such promise then

Was not forgotten ; no, nor unfulfilled ;

For, when we rose, the audible hush that comes

In place of silence, when our feet have left

Some holy place, proclaimed that on the heart

God's dew had fallen, and the soul was full.

Then blithe good-nights and wishings for the
    morrow

Fell fast and thick ; as each to other turned

Some parting message each had found for each.

Then children to their chambers and their
  dreams ;

The servant to his rest ; but we would stay ;

And, gathered in a ring about the fire,

Or where the fire should be on wintry nights,

For then it was the heart of summer-time,

Swayed by some natural instinct, to the hearth,

True altar of the gossip, were we drawn ;

And there we kept the tourney of debate,

With not a pause or resting of the lance

Till lamp flared low and moon was gliding high.

For first we laid the laws of village state ;

How vestries should be guided, how the schools ;

How best to stamp the spawning schisms out ;

How guard the alehouse maelstrom from the reach

Of giddy youth ; what clubs were good or bad :

And even would we venture in our zeal—

Raw trespassers, indeed, on such a field,

As colts let loose upon a garden plot—

To speak how country maidens should be trained,

How taught the tender offices of home,

And how made meet in happy coming years

To be the helpful mothers of their kind.

And then, forsooth, we mounted up apace;

Down-breaking, as we clomb, the tangled growth

Of old abuses ; setting thinkers free

To speak the thing they will, apart from test

Or trammel; opening up the rounds to all

That long to pluck of wisdom's tree, but lack

The generous hand that holds the ladder up

To reach the topmost boughs. And then we passed

From general to particular, and spoke

Of some who had been lodestars in their time,

But now had fallen to the milky way

Of passing merit: prophets in the front,

And seeming vanguard, of a better age ;

Making a visionary splendour shine

Before them, and arousing all our youth;

Now sitting by their fallen thunderbolts

With shattered sceptres lying at their feet,

And scarce an idle lad to stop and hear

Their teaching, if so be they teach at all.

Then poets' names would glide into our talk;

And one would say " we had no poets now:

Since he the Seer of Rydal fell asleep

There had been many babblers in the land

And mocking birds were many in the woods,

But not a solitary nightingale

To sing and make a music of its own."

Whereat there rose a clamour of dispute

To think that one should dare to speak so ill,

And e'en deny the very sweetest voice

That ever minstrel raised amid the choir

Where all are master-singers sent of God.

The hand that touched the sorrow and the sin

Of Guinevere and made them both immortal;

The tongue that framed of grief the holiest hymn

That ever heart uplifted in its loss ;

It could not be his songs were born of earth,

Poor wandering echoes of some earlier voice,

However loud had been the trumpet-tone,

That was, but is not ; they at least might rise

Above the mimic babble of the crowd

That, thick as swarming linnets in the broom,

Make chatter all the day, yet think they lead

God's anthem through the world." So spoke in
      heat,

Yet lifted to the eloquence of truth,

Some champion of these days wherein we live,

True zealot for the worth of those who stand

High in our midst with palm and crown bestowed

By loving hands, while still the prophet's feet

Press on our earth, not waiting for the hour

When in the starry places of their rule

The souls now shining on our later age

Shall be translated to the eternal heights

Whereon the thrones are set and sceptres ranged

For all the kings of thought. Then other themes,

Less lofty, but ennobled by the use

That man may make of sluggard clod and tilth

And all the generous nurture of the soil,

Had claim and place in that wide talk of ours.

Then great, indeed, the Vicar seemed to be—

More silent while we spoke of books and men—

On shifting crops, the worth of this or that,

On steam-ploughs, patent threshers, new manures,

All things, in truth, that make the farmer fat,

And load his daily converse like himself

With unctuous weight and matter. Till at last

So lengthened ran the current of discourse,

And so borne on were one and all of us—

From poets to potatoes, law to lambs,

And many another contrary, passing swift;

So lightly touching all things, gauging none—

That while we sat, nor thought of time or place,

The solemn stroke of twelve was in our ears :

And as some flight of rooks, down settled close

Crop-full among the beanfields, hear the crack

Of gun, however distant, threatening doom,

And straight are up, till all the air is black ;

So, startled in our trespass on the night,

We too were scared and all our council stopped—

Church, State, the village, farming, buried all

In that one sudden avalanche of surprise ;

Ere yet the rousing clock had told its tale,

Like truant children creeping up to bed,

Each one had grasped his fellow and was gone,

With scarce a word of parting as he went.

Then many a morrow after such a night,

And all unwitting of the wordy fray

That made us such sharp wranglers for the nonce,

How pleasantly the peaceful mornings came,

With melody of motion and of life

To woo us to the river or the wood ;

And through the lazy pastures by the Trent,

With cattle standing idle in the stream

And butterflies adoze upon the grass,

We wandered, rod in hand and brisk of heart,

To try an angler's fortune with the trout.

And all among the banner-waving weeds

We watched the grayling in and out the shoals ;

Or saw with wonder how the scurrying dace

Drove like a silver falchion through the pool,

Quick-shaken into oneness in their flight,

With ravenous pike pursuing as they fled ;

And ofttimes on a sudden from the bank

The kingfisher flashed past us, and was gone,

Aye faster than his shadow in the stream ;

Or, slowly paddling in and out the reeds,

The rat swam homeward, searching for his hole,

And scared the huddling moor-hen as he went.

So many were the pleasant sights we saw,

All telling of the summer and its joys,

It little mattered that our creel was light,

And not a fish took notice of the fly,

Though daintily you dropped it in the shade,

Light-falling as a blossom from the bough,

Just where the glimmering green of alders made

The pool beneath them palace for the best

And lustiest of the crimson-spotted tribe.

It was enough to be abroad and breathe

The spirit of the season through our sports,

Without so much as thinking what we willed,

Or straining toward new pleasures out of sight,

For such a fount sprang in our happy selves.

While earth was glad, and we were glad together,

What, then, was lacking to the fullest joy?

This only, that at times we would some friend

Still toiling at his dusty round of work,

And prisoner in close chambers far away,

Had been a happy sharer in our mirth,

And learned the gladdening lesson of the hour.

Or ofttimes, tired of angling, would we stroll,

To that old church across the ample park ;

And dreaming there a lazy hour or two,

Stretched haply on some lichen-crusted tomb,

And looking upward to the mouldered tower,

We heard the clamorous jackdaws shake a chime

So sudden, from the shining ivy-tods,

One almost thought the sculptured fiends that clung

To every coign of that old-fashioned fane

By some strange spell had started into life

And stirred the sleeping belfry with their rout.

And next we paid our homage to the Hall

That, scarce a hundred paces from the church,

With row on row of windows staring blank,

Has seen five centuries of its noble dead

Borne to their place within the chancel vaults,

And still may stare as blank three centuries hence ;

And there awhile we paced the garden-plot,

Eyeing the peacock carven in the yew,

With trim-cut beds of even-measured bloom,

And many another dull device of old :

Till, wakened by the dancing lights o'erhead,

And waving of the chestnuts in their pride,

We cursed the art that dared such monstrous shapes

To thrust before dame Nature in her courts ;

And so we wandered back into the fields,

Rejoicing in the freedom that they gave ;

And there we talked and loitered all the day,

Till homeward with the sailing rooks we went.

And then began afresh the evening round

Of all so dimly pictured in my verse ;

And gladly would I linger out the hours,

With those delightsome memories in the past :

But as,—so oft delayed, so sorely shunned—

The parting came at last,—and quick farewells,

When quickest best, were taken of our host,

The kindly host that seems no longer ours,

So sore a blight has fallen on his home

Now she the guiding star is quenched in night,

And yet another cross that grave-yard holds—

So must it with my fancies and my rhyme ;

For now the gliding pictures fade and melt,

And looking from my chamber cell I see

The waving hands downsettled, and the woods

That made so blithe a flutter while I wrote,

Ay, seemed to turn the pages with their stir,

Gone with the cherished homestead that they girt;

The far-off murmur from the pasture dies,

The children's voices fail within my ears,

The last long shadow from the wall creeps down,

And only dear remembrance stays with me.

MITRE COURT, TEMPLE,
  November, 1868.

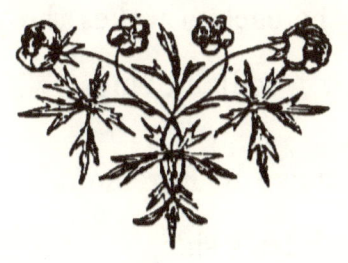

TOM HARTLEY,

A HERO IN HUMBLE LIFE.

WHO knows not Hartley? day by day
    Through every thorpe and town
His busy wheel must work its way
    And hold its old renown.

Nor surer round accustomed eaves
    The wheeling swallow clings,
When first the cuckoo wakes the year,
    And every woodland rings.

Best is he known in Egremont
    On silver Eden's side,
For there full oft upon her banks
    His prowess hath been tried.

By Coniston's delightsome lake,
  By Grasmere's green retreat,
Or where the gentle Rotha runs,
  Beneath old Loughrigg's feet.

By Duddon Grove and Broughton Town,
  And Furness' Abbey old,
Through half the season will he stay,
  There shall his worth be told !

And soon as summer scents the hay,
  Or autumn swells the grain ;
There's many a swain will think of Tom,
  And wish him round again.

For none like he can burnish blade,
  Or edge the mower's pride ;
Through all the length of Westmoreland,
  Or twenty shires beside.

Small stock hath he at fortune's hand,
    As many count their store ;
Yet ne'er a lord in all the land
    Need ask his God for more.

An honest heart that gets him bread,
    A heart that keeps content ;
These are his wealth, and in their stead
    What better may be sent ?

And here ofttime beside the road
    He at his task is seen,
Or yonder where the old elm tree shades
    The dappled village green.

From dawn to dark his wheel is heard
    As blithesome as a bee ;
While here a word, and there a word,
    How briskly gossips he.

To each he gives his golden smile,
    For all are known to him ;
From childhood bright as cherry bloom,
    To old age hoar and dim.

For think not toil, and that fierce strife
    Which sometimes labour brings,
Have blurred the beauty of his life,
    Or lost him happier things.

But rather hath he gained a zest
    From this his hard employ ;
As 'twere a whetstone at the heart
    To give an edge to joy.

And often as the wheel whirrs round,
    While yet he plies his trade,
His ear will catch some sweeter sound,
    Far off his thoughts have strayed.

Perchance his little home-side brook
　　In fancy babbles by ;
Then mark the spring-tide in his look,
　　Spring sunshine in his eye !

Or it may be he walks again
　　Beside some glorious flood,
Where cataracts bellow down the glen,
　　And shake the echoing wood.

For oft before the dawn is up,
　　While stars bestrew the gray,
With steps that chide the laggard sun
　　He hastes upon his way.

And ere the upland dew be dry,
　　Or folded flowers be out,
His hazel rod will arch amain
　　Above the plunging trout.

For well he loves each stately stream,
　And well the noisy rills ;
With every sullen tarn that sleeps
　Amid the brooding hills.

Hence is he dear full far and near
　To every fisher's heart ;
Another Walton given to earth,
　True patriarch of his art.

Yet sometimes thoughts of sterner strain
　Than rod or line suggest
Will drift across the busy brain,
　And harbour in the breast.

Hence holds he truth as clear and good
　As ever fell from pen —
Rare wisdom, by the wayside learned ;
　Ripe knowledge, not of men.

And often while he jogs apace
He weaves a simple song ;
Till many a rhyme of wondrous grace
Will flash upon the tongue.

Some gleams across the memory fly,
Some joy his fancy fills ;
And he must sing, he knows not why,
For all his nature thrills.

So keepeth he for each and all
What best may bring relief ;—
In mirthful mood, good store of jokes ;
In sorrow, honest grief.

Then wheresoe'er my course is run,
Should heaven yet grant me days,
I know no better guide than he
To shape my daily ways.

A Hero in Humble Life.

A trustful heart that takes its lot
 And dares not to repine,
Whate'er of ill it may have got—
 I would such heart were mine.

A hand, it may be, rough with toil
 Where gnarléd veins entwine,
Yet knows no soil of fraud or wrong—
 I would such hand were mine.

An eye that hath the fire of youth,
 Yet keeps the ray divine,
Awake to beauty and to truth—
 I would such eye were mine.

A life that lights our common road,
 Yet still is seen to shine,
Unfailing in earth's dust and din
 I would such life were mine.

Such, Hartley, seem thy hand and heart,
And such thy life to me ;
So thank I God for what thou art,
And what I yet would be.

ONE NOTE WRONG.

BLUE bends the sky above,
  Blue runs the stream below ;
So still, the brooding dove
  Her crooning doth forego.

Nor leaf nor shadow falls
  On all the green hill-side,
E'en to the cuckoo's calls
  Echo but half replied.

So lazy goes the hour,
  The very dragon-fly,
Perched on the dozing flower,
  Moves neither wing nor eye.

Bird, blossom, branch, and stream
　　Are quiet as the air ;
And lying as in dream
　　Earth seemeth passing fair.

Oh, what a hymn divine
　　Breathes from this golden June !
And only this heart of mine
　　Is beating out of tune.

A REGRET.

I.

I MET the maiden that I loved
   One evening on the lea ;
And save a peeping star or two
   All by ourselves were we.
The silken moths flew round about,
   And softly moved the air,
But softlier on my shoulder fell
   The flutter of her hair.
And so we walked an hour or more :
   How swift the minutes sped !
And then we parted—well-a-day,
   What might I not have said ?

II.

I met the maiden that I loved
One sweet May-morn again,
And save the happy Sabbath bells
No sound was in the lane.
But when I looked her in the face
So fast the blushes flew,
No wild-rose blossom in the Spring
Had ever such a hue.
And so we wandered toward the church :
How swift the minutes sped !
And then we parted—well-a-day,
What might I not have said ?

III.

I met the maiden that I loved
Once more in after years,
And as she passed me in the street
I scarce could look for tears.

For by her side a stranger walked,
  And she might be his bride—
But oh ! she smiled not as of yore
  Our darling village pride.
Then most I thought of one still eve,
  Of one May-morn, how sped,
And how we parted—well-a-day,
  What might I not have said !

LINES TO A LADY,

WHO PRESENTED THE AUTHOR WITH AN ORNAMENTAL
ALMS-BOX, PAINTED FOR HIM AT HIS REQUEST.

THANKS for the offering that you send,
    Rare working of the dainty brush ;
Yet shall I wholly thank thee, friend,
    When such sad thoughts upon me rush ?

Our scanty alms are weak, I ween,
    To stem the ills that round us lie :
So deep the shadows fall, unseen
    Our little lanterns droop and die.

From day to day we peer about
    Beside the stream of human woe ;
So noisy is the world's vain rout,
    Unmissed may thousands come and go.

Yet watchers in the furthest creek
    That dents the ocean's boundless shore
Have dreams that lips may never speak,
    Have thoughts that grow from more to more.

And oft the lamp that specks the dark
    From the poor fisher's cabin far
May homeward light some staggering bark,
    And give more hope than moon or star.

Some shipwrecked boy that nearing home
    A moment dreams a mother's kiss ;
Now lashed upon the greedy foam
    May see—and oh, what dawn of bliss !

So is it with our kindly deeds,
    If love light up our cabin here ;
Wherever human sorrow bleeds,
    Wherever falls the silent tear ;

There may the watcher stand and wait
   Unheeded, while the tempests roll ;
But doubtless through the storms of fate
   The still small voice is in the soul.

Some breaking heart will feel the ray
   And grope from darkness into light :
Some wanderer hail the guiding sway,
   Till day-star crown the lagging night.

So gracious seems the gift you send,
   In hope I drop my slender alms ;
If Spring one generous dew-drop lend,
   Some bud drinks in the healing balms.

And if one soul grow strong once more,
   Or one faint heart get nobler power,
Then take the wealth of Ormus' shore
   And tell me which the better dower.

LOVE'S REMEMBRANCES.

I.

SOFTLY fell a lover's words
  In the quiet night :
Never note of sweetest birds
  Brought so rare delight.

II.

Softly fell a lover's looks
  On the wistful face ;
Never moonlight on the brooks
  Brought so rare a grace.

III.

Oh those unforgotten words,
  Thro' the long, long night
Never note of sweetest birds
  Bringeth back delight.

IV.

Oh those unforgotten looks
In these after years !
Never torrent in the brooks
Floweth as my tears.

V.

Oh, that we had never met
In the cruel past ;
Never, never to forget—
Loving to the last.

FOOTSTEPS OF DAY.

I SAW the maiden Morn go forth—and her steps
were soft and still—
To load her golden pitcher at the sunfount on the
hill ;
And, as she bowed her meekly down, the Spirit of
the Day
Stole by, and with his waking breath kissed Night's
dew-tears away.

I saw the maiden yet again, but her looks were
proud and high,
And scarce Earth's bossy shield could bear the fire-
darts of the sky ;

And the bridegroom lay beside her, his giant limbs
    out-spread,
Far in their noon-tide slumber, on his azure-ban-
    nered bed.

I saw the maiden yet again, but her feet were hur-
    rying on,
As 'twere some hooded pilgrim ere yet her journey
    done ;
Quenched was the sunlight in her eyes, and dews
    were on her breast,
While evening flung her purple scarf along the
    shadowed west.

I saw the maiden once again, and as she passed in
    flight
The moon with many a sister star came dancing
    into sight,

And sad and soft on spirit wings as the vision
rolled away,
Fell down the Night's dark curtain on the chambers
of the Day.

LIFE AND LOVE.

I.

LIFE is a garden fair and free,
But 'tis love that holds the golden key;
For hand and heart
Once held apart,
Life's flowers are dashed with storm of sorrow,
And bloom to-day may be blight to-morrow:
Then heedless ever of wind and weather
Let life and love be linked together.

II.

Life is a diamond rich and rare,
But love is the lustre that dances there:
For hand and heart
Once held apart,

Life's jewels grow dim in the breath of sorrow,

And diamond to-day may be dust to-morrow;

Then heedless ever of wind and weather

Let life and love be linked together.

III.

Life hath a fair and a sunshine face,

But love is the beauty that gives it grace;

For hand and heart

Once held apart,

The sweetest cheeks are paled with sorrow,

And blush to-day may be blanched to-morrow:

Then heedless ever of wind or weather,

Let life and love, be linked together.

ORYTHYIA;

A CLASSICAL BALLAD.

AN OLD STORY RUN INTO MODERN RHYME.

NOTE—Orythyia, a daughter of Erectheus, king of Athens, was carried off whilst fording the river Ilissus by Boreas the north wind.

B Y the old Ilissus river
In the amber dawn of day,
Went the maiden Orythyia,
Lightly laughing all the way.

Yonder lies the royal city,
With its towers all ruby-bright,
Like a giant's crown of jewels
Flashing to the early light.

From the lark in heaven above her
 Airy music ripples by,
Till the dancing reeds and lilies
 Seem a-tremble with reply.

Brisk as she that runs beside it
 Runs the river all the while,
Chiming to her silver laughter,
 Sparkling to her every smile.

All that's ever bright and bonny
 Now is up throughout the land,
As if Nature's self were walking
 With the maiden hand in hand.

" Why so early, winsome lady,
 Here upon the plain alone,
Is it that thy pomp and palace
 To the heart have weary grown ?

"Is it that thy maiden fancies
  Loathe the gilded toils of state,
As the prisoned mavis pineth
  For the wild woods and her mate?

"Or may love for some brave spirit,
  Worthy thee, though lowly born,
Lead thee to a place of trysting
  On the threshold of the morn?

"Lady, whatsoe'er thine errand,
  Speed thee, yet remember well
What the royal Seer of old time
  To thy grandsire did foretell.

"Trust not to the treacherous sunshine,
  (Brightly gleams the cruel sword!)
And despite the jocund river,
  Maid, beware the fatal ford."

So some guardian spirit whispered
　Softly on the damsel's ear,
But the air was all so merry
　That she scarcely seemed to hear.

Onward through the laughing meadows,
　Onward through the dewy glade,
Still their sweet communion keeping,
　Run the river and the maid.

See the ford is now before her,
　With its shallows diamond-clear ;
Stepping stones begemmed with mosses
　Cannot harbour any fear.

Ah ! her rose-red foot is trembling,
　And her looks are lily-pale,
For the echo of the Storm-god
　Rings upon the hurrying gale.

Old Ilissus, lashed to fury,
    Headlong tumbles to the sea,
And the heaven, now rent with thunder,
    Clangs with all its winds set free.

But the sweet maid Orythyia,
    Like some flower that none can save,
All bewrapt in storm and torrent,
    Boreas hurries to his cave.

Round her wild winds roar and revel,
    Ceaseless thro' the night and day,
While she ever sits and sorrows,
    " Oh that life had passed away !"

Well the royal seer had spoken,
    Never spake he truer word,
" Maid, beware the wily Storm-god,
    Maid, beware the fatal ford !"

Long they sought her, long they mourned her

   By the old Ilissus' shore,

But the maiden Orythyia

   Cometh homeward nevermore.

AN OLD MAN'S CHRISTMAS THOUGHTS.

I.

IT is not as it used to be
  In years gone by with mine and me :
For then the jolly Christmas came
To boyish spirits all a-flame ;
Then leaping pulses caught the glow
That speaks the spring beneath the snow ;
Then hearts blazed up to full desire,
As blazed the Yule-log in the fire ;
Then foot and fancy danced together,
Nor felt the touch of wintry weather
  In years gone by, gone by for ever,
    Ah, me, for ever !

II.

It is not as it used to be
In years gone by with mine and me ;
For now the common light of day
From these dim orbs has passed away ;
The tell-tale silver threads my hair,
And coldly comes the Christmas air ;
My very heart-beat seems to fall
As echo in some ruined hall ;
For youth, and friends, have flown together,
While I dream here in the wintry weather,
    And sigh for days gone by for ever,
        Ah, me ! for ever !

III.

Oh, dullard heart, that will not hear
The teachings of the vanished year !
Oh, foolish thoughts that cannot see
'Tis better than it used to be !

5

For times gone by so brimmed with mirth,

But leave me weary of the earth ;

There comes no winter to the soul,

And through the mists I hail the goal ;

Where Hope and Faith look forth together,

Nor heed they ought of wind or weather,

Or years gone by, gone by for ever,

I joy, for ever !

AN ANGLER'S IDYLL.

5—2

AN ANGLER'S IDYLL.

WRITTEN FROM CAMBRIDGE TO MY OLD FISHER-
FRIEND, W. DALLBRIDGE, OF LYNMOUTH, NORTH
DEVON.

RIED friend and true, best comrade of
    my sports,
    Would, I were with thee now by plea-
    sant Lyn,
To hear the brown, bright waters leap and laugh,
And see the fern-boughs wave their fairy fans.
Ill seems it, this May-morn to bide at home,
And while the frolic hours go tripping by,
Mope o'er these musty folios of the past ;
For ever and anon the sun peeps in
And flinging careless gold upon the floor

Of these old college chambers where I sit,

Would bribe me forth ; yet little tempts us out

In this flat town, however stuffed it be

With all the ripened wisdom of the world.

Man was not made, I hold, to thrive on dust,

Nor, moth-like, fret the sallow scholar's page ;

And though lost Eden's golden gate be barred,

God still hath given us places for delight ;

Nor wills, I ween, that even poorest wit

Should feed for ever on the husks of thought.

And, oh, what change from our old haunts is here !

What poor, trim fields beside your glorious wastes !

Our river—if so rightly it be called,

Where scarce two boats abreast can hold their own---

Lags lazily, and through the level fields,

With trailing barges slinks away to sea.

While on its banks, fit denizens of the fen,

In long low line the dwarfish willows stand,

And base-born grasses toss their ragged locks :

For never in sweet hush of listening eve,

Nor never under dewy eye of dawn,

When most good anglers love old Isaac's ways,

Was lordly salmon seen to flash his mail

In Cam's dead waters ; even the dappled trout

That breaks to silvery dimple all your streams,

And fills the dark wood pools with leaps of life,

Scarce once in twice ten years will wander here ;

And then, if live he can, his little life

Falls to the treacherous net ; the despot pike,

And all the petty tribes that serve his maw,

Best hold such drear dominions ; nobler kind

Be they of fish or fowl love liberty,

And all the quickening life that freedom brings,

And will not brook such bondage.   Even now

Old times stir in me, and an ampler air

Comes from your breezy moorland ; once again,

With trusty rod, best sceptre in my hand,

Beside the bounding Lyn I wander forth ;

And, oh, how jocund on the eager ear,

Rings out the busy music of the reel ;

While through the fluttered woodlands far away,

O'er many a boulder mossed to green and gold,

And many a winking shallow silver clear,

Runs the fresh river.   Here on every side

From out their lavish leaves, star-primroses,

In loving cluster coyly twinkle forth,

And flush the bank with bloom ; anemones

In cold clear chalice brimming freshest dew,

Pale sorrels, bowed to earth, all blossom-bells,

That on the bridal eve of elfin maid

Ring airy music, else unheard of men ;

Such wealth the woodland showers.   While on the
    air,

Pied moths, and all fair things that love the May,

Are up and busy.   Many and many a time

Can I remember when we sat us down

On yon hoar-lichened crag, that fronts me now,

And while the listless noon stole idly by,

And not a samlet stirred the lazy pools,

Talked o'er our treasures ; told of glorious days

By Barle or Exe, when every creel was crammed,

And in imagination counted o'er

The every spoil that every hour had won.

Hand me the cup—this amber water gleams

Far fairer than the light of all your ales

Or dancing rubies of the bravest wine.

Here would I be and dream the live-long day,

While ne'er a cloud-flake creeps across the blue,

And all the air is witching.   Would I were

Yonder squat ousel, that from stone to stone

Flits daintily, and makes a pleasant seat

Of every emerald isle that gems the stream ;

For well it chirps its little life away,

And leaves our world to wag as best it can.

We cannot hope such freedom ; even now,

Ere yet the merry notes are lost in air,

Hark to the sound, my dream itself has flown,

And all the fairy fancies of my brain,

That in the passing sunshine danced and sang,

Have stolen away and fled. Again that sound—

But not of welcome water—floods mine ear.

And through the antique courts that hem me in,

The thoughtless crowd goes hurrying in to prayer,

And leaves me still brain-weary o'er my books.

TRINITY HALL, CAMBRIDGE,
May, 1861.

AN APPEAL FOR THE CRIPPLES' HOME.

ANOTHER summer, God be praised, has
blessed us as of yore,
And yet another autumn swells the gracious har-
vest store.
Again the teeming city takes its wonted span of
rest,
A gladsome boon to hand and brain that long have
toiled their best;
The eyes that many a lagging month, close watch-
ing soon and late,
Eked out their slender light to make more luxuries
for the great—

E'en they, perhaps, for one short day, may leave
    grim toil alone,
To look the broad sun in the face, and feel it still
    their own.
The aching fingers, weak and worn, that long have
    borne the strain
Of that fierce greed that crusheth one to swell an-
    other's gain,
Perchance a few fleet hours may clasp the tender
    things of life ;
Fair flowers that neither toil nor spin, and know
    not any strife.
And round their path the breeze may blow that
    gives its life to all,
With plenteous gold from heaven's own hand, that
    never made a thrall.
But ye that live afar from want, and eat but what
    ye buy,
That wear what starving sisters weave, but do not
    hear their sigh ;

That know no world without yourselves, and to
such ease attain,

That wish for some new pleasure seems your only
sense of pain.

Ye cannot tell what joy may flood the parchèd
worker's breast,

For whom one day, in all the year, gleams out
amid the rest.

When first he feels the wheel is stayed, the garret-
dungeon fled,

And, joy ! the wide sward under foot, the free sky
overhead.

The very wave, that brimmed with life, comes
leaping up the shore,

Though it but leap as yesterday, and shall leap
evermore ;

Yet seems the while so joyous grown, he cannot
help the thought,

As if it only leapt for him, and all else round were
nought.

The bee that haunts the humming air, the bird
that sails the blue,

It seems ne'er sung so brisk before, nor half so
blithely flew.

Then give him still his idle dream—tho' now it
light the gloom,

Surely to-morrow's sun brings back the garret and
the loom.

Yet not for such I ask an alms, tho' sore must be
the need

Of those that toil the livelong year, and reap such
scanty meed ;

For lonelier pathways yet are found, where darker
shadows fall,

Since some there be, God give them aid ! that cannot toil at all.

The palsied child that helpless lies, and crowds the
tiny cot,

How poor so e'er the father be, must share his
scanty lot.

Its shrivelled hand is cold and dead, and scarce can
    hold the crust,
Which father's toil and mother's moil have won it
    from the dust ;
The little brothers come and go, and bring their
    pence at night,
They are so proud of what they win, it too would
    try its might.
But, year by year, the spring comes back and every
    opening flower
That scents the narrow window-sill is glorying in
    its dower ;
But weary limps the winter by, and weary lags the
    spring,
To one, that like the prisoned lark, but feels the
    broken wing.
And so the generous earth goes round, and strong
    men take their fill,
But, oh ! for those that cannot work, yet have
    earth's cravings still !

The rude cold street where rich men pass, and push
　　their busy way,
Where idle Fashion trips and talks, and lives its
　　little day.
Ah, surely, such is not the soil to nurse this
　　withered bloom,
For kinder were the clasping sod and quiet of the
　　tomb !
That dainty glance, that dare not meet the sordid
　　things of woe,
Has little, save an idle scorn, on homeless want to
　　throw.
And if the kindlier heart should stir, and fain
　　would give with glee,
There's many a greedy knave at hand to wrest the
　　cripples' fee.
'Tis ours to shield these lonely souls, to find a
　　haven still,
Where e'en the shattered barks of life may anchor
　　if they will ;

Some fold amid the cruel world, where healing
waters play,
To bathe the fainting lambs that else will perish
by the way.
For these we plead, and even now, our little port
in sight,
There's many a broken raft afloat that hails the
harbour light.
Our fold is full, yet far and near, comes up from
east and west
The bleating of the weary ones, that yearn to find
a rest.
Then come all ye that count with pride your
garners full of grain ;
A few spare ears is all we ask, and would not ask
in vain.
And if our great God bless your store, and strew
your path with flowers,
Think not that life shall sparkle less for sometimes meeting showers.

Most after gloom we love the light, the sunshine
    follows rain ;
And he that gives to others' need, himself has
    made a gain.
Then Christ be with us, one and all, for He
    alone at length
Can give the crippled heart its balm, and every
    weak one strength.

Note.—Since these lines were written, the "Cripples'
Home," in the Marylebone Road, London, on whose behalf
they were penned, has been much enlarged, but there are still
many poor cripples for whom no suitable home or other
accommodation has been provided. I commend this noble
institution to my readers' best thoughts.

SONNETS

CHIEFLY ON

POLITICAL EVENTS.

1860 TO 1864.

A SONNET.

WRITTEN AFTER THE GREAT VOLUNTEER REVIEW
HELD IN HYDE PARK, JUNE 23, 1860.

ET not the man that saw, forget the day,
Now gathered to the great things
of the past,
When to the strenuous note of honour's blast,
Flinging at once their sordid cares away,
Our sons of trade leapt forth in new array,
Not as of old in jealous ranks combined
To push the paltry profits of their kind—
But through their myriad host, with even sway.
Throbbed the great heart of England. Nevermore
Shall idle whispers of the coming Gaul
Nor any phantom foe our breasts appal;
But through the dear old land from shore to shore,
" Ready, ay ready," is the people's call,
" And come who may, we meet them as of yore."

ITALY IN TRANSITION, 1860.

SUGGESTED BY A BOOK BEARING THE ABOVE TITLE.

SWEET Italy, in this thine hour of need
    Fresh waking from those troublous dreams
      that pressed
So long and sorely on thy loving breast,
As if by some enchanter's magic freed,
Thou seem'st like that fair lady who, we read,
Though long long years in strangest slumber
    bound,
Heard her true lord, and, starting to the sound,
In youth's best beauty hailed her suitor's speed.
Thy bridegroom, long-adored, awaits thee now,
And in his hand the crown of olive leaf
Looks fairer than the laurel on his brow,
Which still is wet with noblest dews of grief—
Therefore take heart and cast sad weeds aside,
For thou art plighted now, a happy bride.

TO MARYAN LANGIEWICZ, EX-DIC- TATOR OF POLAND.

A NOTHER gleam of freedom quenched in
night ;
Another mighty arm upraised in vain :
Yet not for naught ; for surely noble gain
Lives even in loss that springeth out of right.
Thine, Langiewicz, the joy that hailed the light ;
Thine now the pang that feels 'tis lost again,
Yet lives a splendid solace in thy pain
That still shall make thy generous error bright.
Too oft the passionate pulsings of the heart
Outstrip our hand, and nations are as we
When bondage breeds the fever to be free.
Thy Poland called, and thou hast played a part
Not fruitless, though it now should seem to be—
Love waits and suffers, so must liberty.

March 24, 1863.

A CRY FROM THE CAUCASUS.

SUGGESTED BY THE CIRCASSIAN EXODUS.

THE soul of Freedom cannot be subdued,
 Though the mailed heel of tyrants tread her
  down ;
For if that she be thrust from court or town,
Yet hath she higher place and loftier mood—
Lone-sitting in her ancient solitude
Among the eternal mountains, on whose breast
The frown of king or senate may not rest
To fright the royal eagle and her brood.
So seemed it—but to-day, oh infamy !
Her shrine is spoiled, the robber on her throne,
And from the heights of Caucasus the moan
Of her lone children flying to the sea,
Freedom's last refuge now, is in our ears,—
Oh, brothers, shall we give them naught but tears ?

1864.

ENGLAND'S WELCOME TO GARIBALDI.

WHAT worthy welcome can the people pour
  From this free land now every heart
    beats high
Towards him, the foremost son of liberty,
Whose feet so soon shall press our honoured shore?
Surely the vulgar crowd and cheap uproar,
That springs with every breeze of passing fame,
Can add no mite of glory to his name,
That shineth as the stars for evermore.
The eagle, if to earth he bend his flight,
Needs not the warbled homage of the plain;
But rather royal silence is his right,
Lest all too soon he soar to heaven again:
And such a reverent greeting should we pay
To that great soul that is our guest to-day.

April, 1864.

A SONNET.

SUGGESTED BY BRITISH REVERSES IN NEW ZEALAND.

WHAT noise of war, what rumour of defeat,
    Is this that breaks upon our coasts to-day ?
No sound of triumph rising from the fray—
No deeds of might whereat the heart should beat,
And every face be glad in field or street,
As though our own right hands had struck the
    blow.
In England's valiant past it was not so ;
For every blazoned flag in camp or fleet
Then bore high names fore-graven on our souls—
Of conquests that her sons were proud to share,
And trophies hallowed by a people's prayer.
No idle slaughter of barbaric shoals
Then heaped the dripping laurels on our brow,
And mocked the thought of glory ;—shall it now ?

SONNET.

SUGGESTED BY THE APPROACHING PRESIDENTIAL ELECTION IN THE UNITED STATES.

DARK is the land with gathering gloom and
    doubt,

Though parted for the moment seems the rack

Of baleful war, in whose disastrous track

These four long years, in mingled waste and rout,

Have all fair forms and thoughts been blotted out.

And now in this dread pause there comes the lack

Of one strong arm to roll the tempest back,

And bring, though late, the welcome calm about.

God grant that he whom popular vote demand,

May bear, Heaven's purpose wrought, the healing
    aid,

E'en as of old stood Aaron, undismayed

Between the living and the dead to stand,

And, with peace-laden censer in his hand,

Stretch forth and save that so the plague be stayed.

November, 1864.

UNDER THE SEA.

I.

UPON yon summer sea
　　With never a flake of foam ;
Like far sail fluttering free,
　　The wild birds roam.

II.

Above yon summer sea
　　With never a cloud in view ;
Heaven looks adown on me
　　Calm, bright, and blue.

III.

Yet into that summer sea,
  With never a glance of grief ;
Fain would my spirit flee,
  And seek relief.

IV.

For under that summer sea
  With never a cloud he lies—
Waiting ever for me,
  Yet may not rise.

1860.

THE HOME-STREAM.

A VILLAGE RETROSPECT.

FAST runs the stream beside my door
  As in the by-gone years :
But faster run my thoughts before,
  And faster fall my tears.

Along those banks my boyhood strayed
  And hands were linked in mine ;
Ah, many were the pranks we played
  While youth yet seemed divine.

Then would we wander all the day
  And dream the live-long night ;
Our very dreams so full of play
  We scarcely missed the light.

My brothers bathed in yonder pool,
   For it was clear indeed ;
Where now the moorhen holds her rule
   And dabbles in the weed.

Then Harry clomb the topmost tree,
   And Willy swam the flood :
No fish in pond or brook went free,
   No nest in all the wood.

What autumn-nuttings up the glen,
   What wild-flower hunts in May !
The very copse we rifled then
   Is standing corn to-day.

Ah ! now 'tis twice score years since both
   Stood on that bridge, and I
Now turned from one to other, loth
   To give the last good-bye.

Yet while we talked of distant days,
And all that they should bear,
Strange shadows fell before my gaze
And hushed me unaware.

But when we parted, trusting God,
I bid the boys be brave ;
Now one lies under battle sod,
And one beneath the wave.

There stands the school—how oft I drew
My hand from off the latch ;
Half-thinking of some task o'er due,
Half of some coming match.

And then the dear old dame so wise
With glasses on the nose,
We thought she had two pair of eyes
She watched us all so close.

Beneath you yew she sleepeth well,
  It was her chosen place ;
And stranger lips must teach to spell
  And sway the younger race.

Now some trim mistress fresh from school
  Sits in the old elbow-chair ;
Though she be prompt with plan and rule,
  I grieve to see her there.

Sufficient for the simple heart,
  That simple code of yore ;
But they who play the modern part
  Must learn the modern lore.

And there's our sexton : rare old man,
  Thy dealings with the dead,
Though stretching half a century's span,
  Have touched not heart nor head ;

And should the grim taskmaster come
  To call thee in at last,
Though quick to help thy neighbours home,
  Thou wilt not answer fast.

But when God takes me, fain would I
  Be laid in earth by thee ;
For let no village upstart try
  His 'prentice spade o'er me.

The Vicar too 'bides with us yet :
  So long has been his reign,
His every Sunday text is set
  In order on my brain.

'Twas he that marked the cross of truth
  Upon my infant brow,
And his the lips that taught my youth
  Its earliest offered vow.

My dying father blessed his name
　　E'en with his parting breath ;
And may not I, his child, yet claim
　　Such guidance unto death ?

It cannot be my time is long,
　　So many gone before,
And only we of all the throng
　　Stand waiting on the shore.

Oh golden past ! I dare not ask
　　That ought should be withdrawn,
Though bitter seems the evening task
　　Of looking back to dawn.

The present is not wholly vain,
　　Nor future wholly dark,
And though mine eyes are dim, I strain
　　Still forward to the ark.

Our time is short, God's rest is sure,
  Though waiting seem so hard ;
But if so be the soul endure
  It hath its own reward.

Then let the stream run by my door
  As in the former years ;
'Tis dearer for these thoughts of yore,
  And these awakened tears.

VERSES

ADDRESSED TO TWO LADIES WHO THOUGHT IT ADVISABLE
TO SEND TO THE AUTHOR A TRACT ON "SLANDER."

I TAKE the printed page you send,
　　I read it, and, I know not why,
The heart of brother and of friend
　　Is such I cannot lay it by.

I know it was not winged with spite,
　　Yet random shafts may rankle deep,
And idle things, and seeming slight,
　　May stir sad thoughts that will not sleep.

Though shadow of a constant grief
    Had turned to twilight all my day,
Yet surely this were poor relief—
    To sweep my few pale stars away.

Some hope I had by kindly deed,
    Or kindly thought, to make atone,
And so above my utmost need
    To heal some griefs beyond my own.

I know not why it is not so,
    I know not why such hopes were vain,
But surely as the seasons go
    True hearts shall know their own again.

The hands held back in half accord
    Shall yet be warm with friendly fires ;
And tongues now measuring word for word
    Again be quick to kind desires.

The thwarted aim shall yet be true,
  The seeming wrong be understood ;
So is it ever, sweet or rue,
  I take life's gifts and hold them good.

Yet as when cloudlets rest awhile
  High in the heaven's exhaustless range,
Though all the blue horizon smile
  Faint hearts forebode disastrous change.

Thro' all the long delicious noon
  Some shadows of a clouded dawn,
Beyond the breath and bloom of June,
  O'er doubting souls will still be drawn.

So is it with this human life,
  Though hearts be deep as sea or sky :
The shadows of our daily strife
  May never wholly pass and die.

In some still hour when most we feel
    Such joy as peace alone can shed,
How often will strange darkness steal
    From some old care we thought was dead !

Some ghost of a forgotten day,
    Maybe but words too idly spoken,
Comes on us as a cloud in May,
    And all the sweet May-spells are broken.

So is it.—Take the truth, young heart,
    That still has spring in act and word ;
And trust me, no unkindly part
    Was dreamed of : yet I may have erred ;

For surely silly thoughts will stray
    When heart beats high, and mirth is rife,
And tilting in the tourney-fray
    May turn glad pastime into strife.

So sparks that leap with honest gleam
 May fall and scorch some tender flower ;
And spray that crowns the torrent's stream
 May rudely drench my lady's bower.

Yet charge not Nature with the sin,
 Upbraid not rashly flame or tide ;
There's music in the torrent's din,
 There's magic at the warm fireside.

So am I well content to bear
 The burden that your hands have laid ;
In presence of a larger care
 I know that such will soon be stayed.

Cares mould the mingled life we lead,
 They chiefly teach us to be calm ;
And though the heavens be dark o'erhead
 Dear Nature drops her wonted balm.

So can I take the words you send,

   And weigh them more than I can tell ;

For heart of brother and of friend

   Abideth—therefore all is well.

LADY EVELYN'S SORROW;

A BALLAD

OF THE LITTLE GREAT WORLD.

LADY EVELYN'S SORROW.

A BALLAD OF THE LITTLE GREAT WORLD.

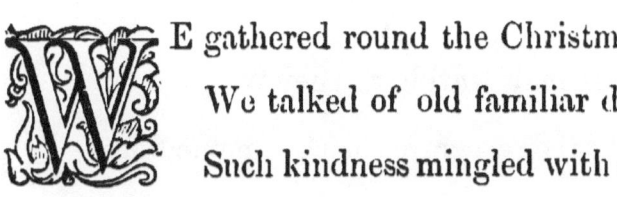 E gathered round the Christmas hearth,

We talked of old familiar days :

Such kindness mingled with our mirth,

For each there fell some word of praise.

Yet far from out the firelight glow

The Lady Evelyn sat apart,

And e'en her beauty seemed to throw

A sense of sadness on the heart.

We looked upon the pale sweet face
   Where girlhood should have blossomed fair,
But over all there ran the trace
   Of some deep sorrow'graven there.

So often when the woods are green,
   And every hedge is bowed with May,
A gleam of snow may yet be seen
   In some still spot beside our way.

The birds may warble as they will,
   The heavens o'erarch with summer blue ;
Yet human hearts will feel a chill,
   And wintry thoughts will rise anew.

Thus on our souls that happy time
   The Lady Evelyn's sorrow lay ;
The one false note in all the chime,
   Yet making all our music stray.

Beside her, gazing to the floor
  As though he read some wizard word,
Stood he whom in the years before
  She took in girlhood for her lord.

In sooth he bore a lofty name,
  Was high in honour through the land ;
And right it seemed that such should claim
  To take the Lady Evelyn's hand.

Fair towered his fame o'er squire and hind,
  With half a county at his call ;
Nor braver welcome could you find
  Than in his old ancestral hall.

There, touched not by the flowing years,
  Good English customs yet were seen :
For rich the feast among their peers,
  For poor the dance upon the green.

And there well-loved, with manly pride,
 Had sire and son upheld their state ;
And worthier home for such a bride
 There seemed not in the reach of fate.

Yet looked the Lady Evelyn sad
 When first he told her of his love,
For vainly would the heart be glad
 If 'tis not prompted from above.

Well might she own his generous worth,
 His noble yearnings for the truth ;
But in her soul she felt the dearth
 Of that which makes the love of youth.

Her eyes might gaze with fond delight,
 Her ears drink in his every word,
But oh ! that one could come in sight,
 And other accents might be heard.

A dream that would not pass away,
    A face that could not be denied ;
These were the thoughts that on her lay—
    She could not be another's bride.

Yet, year by year, her beauty grew,
    And year by year he loved her more,
But should his tongue the suit renew
    Her heart was silent as before.

And still she met him with the air
    Which only lofty natures know,
So gracious, how can hope despair ?
    So calm,—love is not thronèd so.

Then Lady Evelyn faltered long,
    And dared not meet the coming blast ;
But ah ! the world is all too strong,
    And human hearts will bend at last.

*   *   *   *

Then came the taunts of every day,
  Which wear the guise of kindly part,—
The ever pointed word and way
  That slowly sap the grounded heart.

By cares like these her life was worn,—
  The life which had so fairly spread,
Could day have kept the hopes of morn,
  And all the peace that childhood shed.

So Lady Evelyn wed at last,—
  Since worldly friends must be obeyed,
And love was buried in the past,—
  But this was duty—so they said.

Ah ! well if they had never wed,
  Ay well if they had never met—
For better that two hearts were dead,
  Than linked thro' life but lonely yet.

We cannot teach the mountain stream
    To meet and mingle when we will :
A higher hand than ours, I deem,
    Has shaped each tributary rill.

We cannot teach the wingèd seed
    To fall and blossom at our choice—
How should the wind of heaven heed
    Or hearken to our idle voice ?

Then who are these who dare control
    The currents of our human heart,
Shaping some channel for the soul,
    That drains from life the nobler part ?

To push some paltry gain in life,
    Maybe to make much riches more :
These sow the coming years with strife,
    Yet dream they teach love's holiest lore.

*   *   *   *   *

Then years rolled on—her life was spent
   As are the lives of thousands more ;
While circling seasons came and went,
   But never happier burden bore.

With sad, still steps, she moved and wrought
   The little tasks of every day:
No duty dared she hold for nought,
   For wife must own a husband's sway.

But now the smile which shone of yore,
   As sunshine on the early leaf,
Had faded—to the young heart's core,
   So inly fell the blight of grief.

The hall beneath her gentle sway
   Upheld its more than ancient state,
And never pilgrim passed that way
   But left his blessing at the gate.

Lady Evelyn's Sorrow.

High blazed the banquets in the Yule,
    Such stately feasts were never seen ;
For who could mingle wild mis-rule
    In presence of so rare a queen?

The garden-walks ablaze with flowers,
    In terrace sloped about the hall ;
And there full oft in summer hours
    She wandered, loveliest of them all.

And if that one had met her there
    Slow-pacing in the still twilight,
Well might he deem a form so fair
    Some spirit of the gracious night.

So lonely bright her beauty shone,
    So lonely sweet were all her ways,—
Her very shadow on the stone
    Seemed even too fair for mortal gaze.

But over all the shade of grief,
   Which spoke the brooding sorrow, fell :—
Nor feast, nor flower, could bring relief,
   Heart only said—it is not well.

Her husband—well she styled him Lord,
   His very silence spake command—
Still as of old by all adored,
   Rose ever higher in the land.

His voice—loud only for the right—
   In council shaped the high debate,
Nor lacked his hand the answering might
   To steer the course of house and state.

So honours ripened day by day,
   Till from the topmost round of fame
It seemed that his great deeds should lay
   Foundation of some noble name.

A name that in the distant years
  Should speak the long-emblazoned line—
As yonder planets' gleaming spheres
  Proclaim the sun from whence they shine.

So seemed it—but that richer gift,
  Than gold, or fame, his God denied,
That living link which yet might lift
  His soul to her, then more than bride.

Alone with all life's clustered gain
  His idle grandeur seemed to soar ;
Like some far palm tree on the plain,
  With none to share its golden store.

The last and greatest of his race,
  What matter how his end might come ?
Mid all the blaze of pomp and place,
  Hope had not where to find a home.

Maybe the cradle of a child
   Had proved the holiest shrine on earth,
Could heart to heart be reconciled,
   New-born above the common birth.

Maybe, with such had passed away
   That memory of an earlier love,
Which though in wifely breast it stay,
   No mother's heart hath power to move.

Then all the jarring notes that erst
   Disturbed the sounding psalm of life
Had mingled in the one great burst
   Of concord, sweetest after strife.

Then might the rest for which they yearned
   Have drawn their natures into one ;
Life's truest crown had then been earned,
   The tumult passed, the conquest won.

But in the wiser will of Heaven,

   Though strange to our weak thought it seem,

The boon so prayed might not be given,—

   Still flowed their lives' divided stream;

Still stood the gap 'twixt heart and heart,

   Which meeting hands in vain would span ;

And years but seemed to widelier part

   The lives where true love never ran.

The storms of grief may burst and die,

   The tempest of the soul grow still ;

But if the fount of life be dry,

   Who shall the broken cisterns fill ?

Though well we wear the masks of form,

   And smile in fashion with the rest,

We kill not so the gnawing worm

   That wastes the heart within the breast.

Hence on our souls that happy time
　The Lady Evelyn's sorrow lay ;
The one harsh note in all the chime,
　Yet making all our music stray.

No cloud nor shadow gathered near,
　Our thoughts ran all to merry tune ;
And laden with the season's cheer
　December stole the warmth of June.

But while with song the minutes sped,
　And many a goodly tale went round,
There rose a shriek as o'er the dead,
　And then the Lady Evelyn swooned.

A name struck out in random talk,
　A name of one that was not there,
Had bowed the blossom on the stalk
　And sowed with blight the Christmas air.

She heard as one that, far from home
    In some strange land beyond the seas,
Has chanced in burial-place to roam,
    Unwitting 'neath its cypress trees.

And there in dear familiar guise
    Some name stands graven on the stone,
And through the stream that floods his eyes,
    A vision flashes and is gone.

So that one name within her ears,
    Though ringing ceaseless in her thought,
Bore back the long-departed years,
    And with them all their burden brought.

For one had said he went away,
    And cared not for his life or fame ;
Some spell upon his spirit lay—
    But what had she in such a name ?

For years the claspèd truth could hide,
   With later memories clustered round :
Yet at this goodly Christmas tide,
   In one small word, the key is found.

So strangely in an idle hour
   When life-long cares have kept their tale,
Some seeming trifle hath the power,
   Beyond our wills to rend the veil.

Oh last drop in the brimming flood !
   Oh last flake in the avalanche !
Farewell to yonder towering wood,
   Farewell, farewell, to flower and branch !

Oh heart that these long years could make
   So lonely in their crushing yoke,
Shall now thy pent-up fountains break
   Beneath this seeming lightest stroke ?

So short the span that yet remains

    Between thy bondage and release,

Couldst thou not spare him all the pains

    That wait the severing of his peace?

Nay, tax not now her soul with guilt

    We may not chide, though weak she seem:

The life-blood of her heart was spilt

    For nought, and shall not one redeem?

In vain we raised that drooping head,

    In vain we spoke familiar words;

The magic from the harp had fled,

    Who then might wake the silent chords?

One moment ere the soul had flown,

    We watched, if haply hope could live,

And then, heaven's music in its tone,

    A voice fell on us, " I forgive !"

And now no more those lips are moved—
  Death's signet on that cold white brow :
This only know we, once she loved,
  Maybe that love is perfect now.

So Lady Evelyn heard and fell
  And wearied spirit found its rest :
To us it seemeth ill or well,
  God only knoweth it is best.

Then parting from that Christmas hearth
  Each went his way with silent tread ;
Only the host that ruled our mirth
  Stayed—speechless gazing on the dead.

THE NEW CRUSADE.

AN APPEAL FOR THE UNEDUCATED POOR.

IN the dead of the winter night,
    As I lay on my couch awake,
There fell, as it seemed, a light,
    And I heard a voice that spake.

And it seemed, but I know not why,
    The voice of Him that died,
On the Holy Mount of Calvary—
    Jesus the crucified !

Yet with half-reluctant air,
    I turned on my pillow, and said :
" Speak, Spirit, what message you bear,
    Is it news from the living or dead ?"

And the Spirit answered again :

"O creature troubled and crossed,
Surely I died in vain—
For my lambs are straying and lost !

"In the crush of your proud great city,
So full of revel and scorn,
Have you neither place nor pity
For the little ones weakly and lorn ?"

"They know not their way in the shadows,
Though Wisdom still cries to be heard ;
Far better the marsh and the meadows,
The life of the bee or the bird !"

Then I said—"O Lord, I am thine,
And wait but the word from Thee ;
But why are thy looks divine
So searchingly turned on me ?"

Then he spake, and with kind command,
　　His words as the dew came down—
"Brother, the day is at hand,
　　Lay hold on the Cross and the Crown !

"Behold as I pass thro' your streets,
　　My watchmen away or asleep ;
And for ever there come the bleats
　　Of the wand'ring desolate sheep.

" From the heat of your stifling alleys,
　　Grim gardens of fever and pain ;
From the very green of your valleys ;
　　Far away from the stress and the strain ;

" From garrets seething with leaven
　　Of idleness, folly, and sin,
Where the only glimpse of my heaven
　　Is the stars that look shudderingly in ;

" From all the waste-places of plenty,

 From wretchedness deep as the grave,

They call you ! Go forth, I have sent you,

 Go forth in my spirit and save !"

So spake He, and speaking He vanished,

 And I tell but the vision to-day ;

But when from this heart shall be banished

 The voice that has shown me the way ?

Oh. brothers and sisters mine,

 In the dead of your winter night,

Should the self-same spirit shine

 And utter such words of might —

Wait not for the bigots and schemers,

 Still fighting for sway in their schools ;

Heed not all the profitless dreamers,

 Asleep o'er their systems and rules.

There is work for the hands that are willing,

  And trophies for hearts that are true.

See now ! the dark places are filling

  With beacon-lights kindled anew.

Go forth ! They are far from the fold,

  In their wretchedness black as the grave,

While the Shepherd calls as of old,

  " Go forth in my Spirit and save !"

A FACE.

DEAR face, so sweet, so calm, so sad,
    Unasked, I see thee gliding near.
Now all the world is fair and glad,
      Why art thou here?

When first the year begins to wake,
    Thy shadow falls on flower and leaf,
Till every blossom seems to take
      A touch of grief.

Sweet face! thy beauty brings a shade
    Between the twilight and the moon;
Almost my spirit shrinks, afraid,
      In nights of June.

Calm face ! thou risest in the hour

    When plunging tempests have their will ;

I thank thee—near so sweet a power

    My heart is still.

Sad face ! there is no hour of mirth

    To me or fellow-reveller given,

But thou dost breathe on things of earth

    The balms of heaven.

Dear face ! so sweet, so calm, so sad,

    Unasked, I see thee gliding near.

Though all the world is fair and glad,

    Stay with me here.

SONNETS

ON

GENERAL TOPICS.

SELF-HELP.

A SONNET WRITTEN AFTER READING MR. SMILES'
BOOK WITH THE ABOVE TITLE.

ORK on, hope on,—there's not a page
but cheers
With some high deed in lowliest cradle
born,
Some light now quenchless struggling toward the
morn,
Some arch-apostle erst baptised in tears,
So surely grows the meed of toilsome years.
Not on proud wing do holy angels rise,
But step by step the ladder scales the skies ;
And wouldst thou, worm of earth, in idle scorn
Leap to the highest heaven of honoured art ?
Nay, rather in the fields our fathers trod
Put hand to plough and bravely wake the sod,
Well pleased if from the fulness of her heart
Earth grant thee knowledge, and the smile of God
Light on thy treasure, then in peace depart.

OUR FAIRY LAND.

SUGGESTED BY THE WORKS OF HANS C. ANDERSEN.

WHERE lies the fairy-land so loved of yore ?
 This busy age, methinks, must rudely jar
The lily bells of Oberon's gliding car,
And day by day grim Labour craves for more
Of those fair fields that Fancy roved before.
Yet if so be that elves have passed away,
Lost in the light of Reason's fuller ray,
Yet lives the spirit on, nor wanders far ;
For if the kindly soul interpret well,
In every tender thought of heart and home,
In each high hope, whence generous actions come,
Some power of earth, or air, has woven spell,
And so about our paths good fairies roam.

EVERY-DAY RELIGION.

WRITTEN IN A COPY OF THE REV. J. CAIRD'S
SERMONS.

NOT alway 'mid the blaze of Sinai's height
    Went forth the word ; and to the prophet
    mind
Above the fire, the earthquake, and the wind
That still small voice maintained its heavenly might.
He too that once in godliest garb of light
Before the chosen three transfigured shone
Did, also toward Emmaus journeying on,
Talk by the way, and then they learnt aright.
Hence in no high sequestered world of thought
Where only angels soar our worship lies,
But on whatever field the fight be fought,
On this vexed earth where man yet lives and dies,
There, morn by morn, God's benison may be sought,
And duty fitly done best wins the skies.

HOME TRAVEL.

SUGGESTED BY THE WORKS OF MR. WALTER WHITE.

ILL-GUIDING seems to me the fickle hand
    That now o'er perilous peaks of Alpine snow,
And now in strange new places, to and fro,
Points out the pilgrim's path. Our quiet land,
If giddy souls would rightly understand,
Hath pleasant haunts for all, and they who go
Wherever faintest breaths of fashion blow,
Might by their own home door rare sights command;
For where the heart leads there true travel lies,
And then do love-links bind us everywhere,
While, called at will before fond gazing eyes,
Such thoughts and fancies fill the charmèd air,
That every leaf that trembles in the breeze
Swarms with sweet memories thick as summer-bees.

SONNET,

ADDRESSED TO AN ENTHUSIASTIC CO-OPERATOR.

FAINT not, though still the world be bent on
    gain,
The present seeming as the selfish past.
High thoughts are not mere thistle on the blast,
But somewhere surely sow the future grain;
And hopes to-day hereafter shall attain
To helpful good. Our very births are cast
In such a law, that, while her anguish last
The mother knows but of the passing pain—
Therefore work on, though thick the shadows fall,
And groping in the twilight seems so sad ;
Somewhere the golden keys behind the pall
Await us—seek them ; earth shall yet be glad,
When all the pathways to the common good
Are opened, we shall enter as a flood.

A SONNET.

WRITTEN AFTER A VISIT TO A POPULAR PLACE OF
AMUSEMENT.

HOPES once we had that riper times were nigh,
　　And fondly deemed ourselves would hail the
　　day
When fruitful wisdom seasoning all our play
Might in the idlest hour, however high
Beat the mad pulse of mirth, have lingered by :
And while the young heart leaped, as leap it may,
Lifting our souls above mere sensual sway,
Have left us less the slaves of ear and eye.
Yet seems to-day small bettering of the past,
Since every trifling mood will have its toy ;
And so ill-schooled are we for nobler joy,
And in such mould are freakish fashions cast,
That he who walks a rope has rich employ,
While steadfast toil too oft but reaps the blast.

A SONNET,

ADDRESSED TO ONE WHO SAID THERE WAS NO NEED
OF ANY MORE POETRY BEING WRITTEN.

YOU say that now there is enough of song,
    Enough of music floating on the earth,
So bounteous is the store, so rare the worth
Of those full notes that thro' the ages long
From poet's graves into our memory throng
As fresh as in the hour that gave them birth :
And surely, God be thanked, there is no dearth
Of strains that melt or make the spirit strong ;
Yet, though the night hang all her stars on high,
No less the glow-worm lights her slender ray ;
Nor less the linnet on his covert spray
Pipes, though a thousand songsters mount the sky :
So must full hearts have utterance, and in rhyme
Breathe out their music to the end of time.

SHAKESPEARE WORSHIP.

SUGGESTED BY CERTAIN FOOLISH PERFORMANCES
AT THE TER-CENTENARY CELEBRATION OF SHAKE-
SPEARE'S BIRTH IN 1864.

HIGH heaven, the depth of ocean, and the sight
    Of that great orb whence all our seeing flows,
Are but as symbols dim and outward shows
Beside the beauty, majesty, and might
That from the cradle of one mortal wight,
Now never to be quenched or lost below,
Dawned on the world three hundred years ago,
And still are broadening to the perfect light.
Then who are we that with our paltry art
We hang our little lanterns at the noon,
And think when we have played the mummer's part
That Shakespeare's self is richer for the boon?
Enough for us that we may own his sway,
For fitting tribute is not ours to pay.

THE LOSS OF PURITY.

OH, for the loss of childhood's purity !
    For who shall bid the fallen dew arise,
Though only in some wild-flower's cup it lies,
To mount afresh into its native sky ?
The taint of earth is on us till we die ;
And all the holy tears from angel eyes,
Though born of heaven's divinest sympathies,
Blot not the record from our memory.
So deep, so dark, the closing shadows fall,
"Dear God," we cry, "shall daylight break no
    more ?
Behind us, far away, home-voices call,
But we are ever drifting from the shore,
And who will help us ?" Peace, poor heart forlorn !
Look up, the night is darkest towards the morn.

10

OUT OF WORK.

A HUMAN PLEA FOR EXTENDED EMIGRATION.

THE winter is round again—
　　Will Winter and Want ne'er part ?—
And the frost is back on the pane,
　　And the frost is back at the heart.

There's starlight up in the sky,
　　And there's firelight over the way ;
But the stars are all too high,
　　And fires are for those that pay.

I tramp in the cold grey morn,
　　I tramp when the daylight lags,
'Till my bleeding feet are torn,
　　On these merciless London flags ;

And I stare as the folk go by,

   Their faces so cold and hard,

That I think of the stones that lie

   In the hell of the workhouse yard.

" Dear soul, I have nothing to give,"

   Is all that the best reply :

" How is it you care to live,

   There is nothing to do but to die."

And others scoff as they walk—

   " Oh, yes ! we know you of old ;

You have plenty of pitiful talk,

   And brass is the beggar's gold."

Yet I ask neither silver nor bread,

   I merely ask for a wage :

But somehow, they say, the markets are dead.

   And it's only the fault of the age !

Still I read that far away,
Somewhere in the glowing West,
There are realms without rent to pay,
And the labourer's lot is the best.

And oft in the long dark hours
I dream of the tales they tell,
Till the breath of the prairie flowers
Steals over me like a spell,

And I smile on my own broad farm,
While the children around me call,
" Now, father, we fear no harm,
There's room enough for us all."

But I wake too soon to my pains,
And, waking, I hear once more
The din of the market-wains,
Heavy-laden with rich men's store.

They pass with the music of birds,
　　And I hear men shout as they go ;
But the very cheer of their words
　　Falls into my heart like snow.

Still I ask for the goods of none,
　　And I ask for the alms of none ;
But murmur " Thy will be done,
　　If it be that I starve alone."

For I trust that the good God knows—
　　And they tell me His ways are just—
That the winter will bring its woes,
　　That some must fall in the dust.

Yet ever I tramp and strive
　　For the labour that will not come,
For the loaf that keeps alive,
　　And the hope that makes a home.

Are they never to come again ?
 Ah, me ! for that land in the west !
Is there none that will lead the train
 That takes us away to our rest ?

We are willing, longing to go,
 And the far land calls in her strength,
" Come, children, why perish ye so ?
 Come lie in my bosom at length."

Yet ever the cry goes up,
 Till it sounds as a tale that is told—
" Dear mother, this agony cup
 Is more than our hands can hold."

" We yearn for your goodly dower ;
 And over the Western Sea,
The gospel of youth and power
 Is bidding us all be free.

Out of Work.

" But how shall we quit our place,
    Though it's only these icy flags ;
And how shall we win the grace
    That is waiting even for rags ?"

Ah, me ! with hearts so strong,
    And good men high in the land,
To think that the taint of the pauper throng
    Seems worse than the felon's brand !

Yet surely the worst is past ;
    We have waited so long in vain,
That our very souls are aghast,
    And hope is akin to pain.

Then back to the workhouse gate,
    For there's starlight still in the sky,
And they tell me England is great,
    With thousands worse off than I !

MEMORY.

A FRAGMENT.

DEAR memory, most divine of dowers,
That shadowest all our present with the past,
That cheerest Winter with the gleams of Spring,
And wakest living music in the soul
From echo of sweet voices hushed on earth !
What vigil should our every fancy keep
To guard thy records spotless to the end ;
To feed thine altar flame and hold our hearts
Fit shrine and pure for thy virginity !
Thou holdest all the thousand keys of life,
Opening the silent chamber of the heart
And thridding all the avenues of thought,

Whence issue forth the buried shapes of joy

Or grief, and all that moved us in the days

Of that sweet youth that shall return no more ;

Therefore we needs must treasure every thought

That still is fresh with innocent delight,

That still recalls enjoyment unalloyed

With any earthly touch of shame or sin,

Gathering again the dew upon the soul,

As though the gracious manna fell anew

From God's right hand upon our daily paths,

And we were free to gather—all so rich

Are thy good gifts, divinest Memory !

RESTING PLACES.

I.

THERE is a path beside the corn,
 And when the fields were yellow,
That pleasant path beside the corn
 Had never match nor fellow.
How often there we two have walked
 In many a past September !
Methinks of plighting troth we talked,—
 Dear Alice, dost remember ?

II.

There is a place beside the fire,
 And when the lamp was lighted,
How oft that place beside the fire
 Held two young hearts united !

Then little recked we of the threat
  Of dolorous cold November;
'Twas always Summer when we met,
  Ah, me! when I remember!

III.

There is a place within the heart
  Than path or fireside dearer,
And toward that place within the heart
  I would the guest were nearer.
Yet oft I dream it filled by you,
  Then welcome, drear December!
But whether such good dreams come true,
  Dear Alice, dost remember?

FALLEN, NOT LOST.

"LOST ! who said it ?   Oh, no !
  Is God then robbed of his own ?
Surely a voice shall go
  From the king where he sits alone ?

" Say you a jewel fell—
  And ye know not now where it lies—
Out of my heaven, to dwell
  In depth of the seas or the skies ?

" The crown of my glory fails,
  Though but one of all be away :
Somewhere the noontide pales,
  There is loss in my courts to-day.

" In earth that breathes at my feet,
   Tho' the rain of its tears fall fast,
Seek, if there you may meet
   With my treasure, speed on the blast,

" Over the seas of snow,
   Over the waste of sand,
Wherever the free winds blow,
   Wherever the mountains stand.

" Seek when the morning wakes,
   And soon as the sun be up :
Where the lights of river and lakes
   Flash as the wine in the cup.

" Seek in the sweet still eve
   When the flowers are hanging their head,
And the shadows come up and weave
   A pall for the day that is dead.

" Seek in the city gloom
    When the multitudes fail for breath,
And the little ones pine for room
    In darkness deeper than death.

" Wherever the cry comes forth
    Of creatures longing for rest,
Seek for it—South or North,
    Ye shall not fail in your quest."

This is the voice of God
    If one of his children stray.
We that are born of a clod,
    Judge we better to-day ?

We that crouch in our place
    If shadow of change come by,
Though it be but a father's face
    Turned on us out of the sky,—

We that toil at his feet,
  And crush out our lives for gain,
Making each valley and street
  Red as the hands of Cain,—

We that know not to-day
  Whether to-morrow shall be ;
Hither and thither, as spray
  Tossed on an infinite sea.—

Shall we judge of another,
  Giving him scourge or crown,
Sending sister or brother
  Into our hells with a frown ?

Little we know of ourselves,
  Fumbling a knot in the shade :
Are we angels or elves,
  Or why at all were we made ?

What is birth that is first,

   And what is death that is last?

Why is the fair earth curst,

   Where are the future and past?

What is sin but a cloud?

   Whence has it come?—who knows?

Why should beauty be proud,

   Or goodness blush as it goes?

Who hath seen the hereafter?

   Who come back with the tale,

Bringing us weeping or laughter?

   And how shall our lives avail?

These are the things I ask,

   And simple and plain they seem:

Yet as we sit to the task,

   Passing away in a dream,

Answer me one, if you can,

    Though others come as a host ;

Then if you will, oh man,

    Tell me a brother is lost.

FRIEND OR LOVER ?

YOU ask me to wed you, oh, little I ween
    You fathom the thoughts in my heart ;
For deep lies the sorrow that cannot be seen,
    But never on earth shall depart.

One loved me, and girlhood was happy with love,
    Ay happy as birds in the May ;
He came like a vision sent down from above :
    Like vision he vanished away !

Oh ! bright was the morning that took him from
      home,
    The bonniest boy in the fleet ;
Oh ! sad was the morrow that broke o'er the foam,
    And flung him a corpse at my feet.

Full long have I honoured and loved thee as friend,

    And still but as friends we must be !

And the hand which you hold shall be true to the

    end,

    But my heart is there under the sea.

A SONNET.

ADDRESSED TO A FAVOURITE PAPER-KNIFE.

FAIR gleams my ivory falchion's honoured
    blade—
With ne'er a dint to tell how oft I wield
Its trenchant might o'er many a fruitful field,
That else un-won had slumbered in the shade,
And oh! what far and fair campaigns we made
Whether o'er Law's Sahara to advance,
Or in some sweet Arcadia of Romance
Cleaving a pleasant path through bower and glade!
So, for a while in welcome truce to thought,
I range at will o'er every open page,
And musing on past fields so keenly fought,
The mind afresh makes ready to engage—
And once again I grasp thee for the strife,
Thou best Excalbur!—my paper-knife!

WITH A FINE LADY IN 1870.

SCENE :—A LONDON DRAWING-ROOM.

WITH A FINE LADY IN 1870,

IN A LONDON DRAWING-ROOM.

GOOD morning, madam ; 'tis a pleasant
day,
And very cheerful is this summer
time,
Here as we sit, away from all the noise
That makes our city lives so hard to bear.
Yonder the china vase of mignonette
Breathes sweetly, and the idle curtain lace
Flaps lazily at every passing stir :
While roses from your gardens at the Hall
Have showered their wealth to make your London
gay ;

And little miss you of the country stores,

Or all the thousand joys that come with Spring.

Of course, you leave your little ones at home,

You leave them with the lady whom you hire—

French, music, drawing, and a human heart,

At forty pounds a year ; and even now

I see them playing in their baby glee

Among the daisies and the meadow-sweets,

Taking the golden moments as they rise

Nor heed the sullying touch of times to come.

You never saw town-children in their homes,

Nor climbed a garret staircase in the East ?

(Excuse me, but that velvet's very rich :

The rose-leaf fallen from your hand will stain it.)

Their little ones are not so very fair,

And the pinched cheeks have lost the early bloom :

For bread is not so common thereabouts,

As cake and peaches to your darlings' lips.

Perhaps some day you'd like to visit one,

And see these regions where our workers live :

Your carriage with its shining greys will flash

A wonder and a glory in the eyes

Of simple folk, who seldom catch a glimpse

Of any grandeur save a passing hearse,

With all the tinsel pomp of furnished woe.

You see the poor in country cottages?

And labourers say the Squire is very kind,

And so's his lady.　You will read to them

Some chapter from the book that all men love,

Or little tales writ out in baby style,

Well suited for the poor, and given them free,

That teach 'tis good for folks to keep their place

And worship God in quiet; from your pew

(What sleepy cushions you have planted there!)

You see them; all are tenants of the Squire,

And all are very humble as they pass,

Each pulling down his forelock as he goes,

As suits the House of God; and then at Christmas

Your butler, plumper than a bishop, sows

Your tickets far and wide—how sweet it is

To sit at home, beside the roaring fire,

And read of all our bounty to the poor !

Somehow there must be rich and poor, no doubt,

If otherwise, what could a poor man do

In want of work ? the logic's plain enough !

A thousand acres in your park, you say ;

How many in the little garden-plots

That ring those low-browed huts along the road,

You cannot say ?   Ah, me ! what curious tricks

Our memory plays when pride and fancy meet

Above our lowly duties day by day.

I doubt not, Hodge, has bacon once a week :

And e'en doctors, who have said so much

About the common wants of ailing men,

Scarce think it well that eating over-much,

Is good for country hinds.   You dine off plate ?

An heirloom in your family, perhaps,

Taken, I hear it said, by one who lent

Some money, years ago, to a poor.duke

Who kept too much of state, and lost his all ;

A bad example ! but these doctors say

That many little children in the land

Die oft from want of air, and some of food ;

It may be, therefore, though I say not so,

(Being but a thinking man, that speaks his mind,

Not born as some to make the people's laws

With wisdom filtered thro' a spendthrift sire,)

That if some leavings from the hall went down

To feed the little ravens in the road,

That holloa, as the gay barouche rolls by,

'Twere well for all.   I am a Socialist,

I think you said.   That is a strange long word.

Think you, you know the meaning of the same ?

For terms, like these, are tossed from ladies' hands

With all the pretty scorn you wield so well,

And shuttle-cocks, however lightly winged,

Have blinded men ere now ; myself have seen

Great hearts sore-stricken by the easy sting

Of idle minds, that have no time to think.

There was a certain teacher years ago

Who taught some lessons, not all out of date,

Somewhere about the shores of Jordan, and the

    towns

Of Judah.   Churches, were not rented then ·

With seats for rich men at two pounds a year ;

And if I rightly read the words he spake,

For men have rudely wrenched the texts, I hear,

He said, " How hardly shall the rich on earth

Enter God's Kingdom ?"   Heaven's our version's

    phrase.

I thank you ; pray correct me if I err,

Perhaps I have not read my Bible page

So close as you before the morning meal

And after evening ; (family prayers are good,

And keep one's servants used to regular ways).

Again I find it written, " If a man

Ask of thee, turn not thou away ; if coat

He need, give him thy cloak as well."   But times

Are changed, and nigh two thousand years of

    grace

" Have made a world ill-suited to such laws.

" Christ did not mean so much !" My thanks again,

Christ was the teacher whom I spoke of ; strange,

How well you ladies can remember names !

But to retrace the teaching of my texts.

Are there no poor in this good land of ours,

" So radiant as it is with gospel light ?"

(I take the phrase from one I heard last week :

Thump on his velvet desk with gouty hand,)

Are there no little children in our lanes ?

Of whom One said of such His kingdom was ?

The same authority : again you're right.

Are there no fallen women in the street ?

I fear you think me very vulgar now,

Such things are seldom talked in drawing-rooms.

Correggio's Magdalen, on your walls, may be,

(For which the Squire has paid four thousand pounds,

Though some have dared to call it but a daub),

Puts no such questions.   You subscribe, you say,

To several refuges ; how wonderful

It is to see the poor pale creatures come,

(Soiled as that bunch of wild hedge-roses cut

Into your wire-work bowl, to grace a rout,)

And gather in the chapel once a year !

That secretary too, how quick he is,

Showing the patrons what a wond'rous change

Comes over all the inmates—in The Home,—

Some twenty pounds, a-piece, has done it all,

(You saw his last long letter in the " Times ?")

And every year he has more work to do.

" Look, madam, pray,—how clean and neat they are,

How happy in their quiet morning dress,"

And yet you say the sight is somewhat sad.

You would not wish your younger sister Blanche,

" Just out," I think that is the phrase you use,

To share those glances, wear those sweet wan eyes—

You think it best they have a hospital—

Such creatures could not come to proper homes.

Besides there is the ' example,'—did I hear

Some story once about a certain squire,

That had a letter on his wedding-day

Dropped at the altar-rails—ill-written enough,

Yet somehow read with eager haste, and stuck

Into the inmost pocket, out of sight?

Something about a poor strayed wretch that came

And talked so wildly at your old church door,

About her beauty and her babe? 'tis strange,—

The squire is chairman of the sessions now,

Leader in all that's good; well-known for miles

As the best shot,—the Bishop's closest friend;

Only last year the Bishop stayed a week

At the hall,—tired out with battling in the Lords,

And took such interest in the village folk,

Knew every child about—and swore, I mean

Expressed a curious thought—that one pert thing

(That met him in some cottage on the heath

Where the poor dame lives rent free, as I hear,)

Was the exact image of the squire, as shown

In that sweet picture taken years ago,

When fresh from Eton in his cricket suit—

Ridiculous suggestion of the Bishop !

And nothing to the point, you say my talk

Was all about poor women, and I sprawl

Away to such weak gossip—I return,

And many pardons for my foolish plights.

You want to have some facts? I give you one—

Ten thousand women on your streets, at least,

Were once as pure as you.   How well you keep

That dancing rose upon the happy cheek !

What are they now ? mere offal, lilies crushed

And trampled by the feet of busy men,

Who have short time to parley, less to preach.

You give them tracts ? how very good you are !

Did'st ever see a fledgling on the ground,

Born late, when all its tribe were winging south,

How much of help the wheeling swift could give,

That shot a moment down to see its kind,

And then was off again ?   Soft hands, that touch,

And in the touch have healing ; looks that speak

More than the wisest sermon in the world,

However steeped in nineteen centuries' lore ;

Eyes that are stars of hope and lamps of love,

And lips that rightly tremble as they teach,

These have you—will you give your sisters these ?

If so your gold shall have another stamp

Than that of Cæsar—maybe face of Him

That stretched the piercéd arms on Calvary,

And made His sorrow more than all men's store,

Shall bless thee.   Have I spoken cruel things ?

If so, the heart is cruel when it loves,

And tears are saltest when the fount is strong.

Bear with me, madam ; I have much to say,

Yet know too well the crushing weight of use,

And all the dear deceits that come with ease,

To blame you, if you set me down a bore,

One of those strange young men, how many such,

Who think somehow the world has gone astray,

(High God forgetting purpose for an hour,)

And wants a little righting now and then ;

Somehow the sea has shaped its course amiss

And needs a first-class man to guide it back ;

The stars have slipped their orbits in the sky ;

The sun has proved himself a poor wan thing—

Perhaps a mere reflector like the moon,

And wants re-kindling.   As for brother-man,

Born, as they say, some sixty centuries back

And ruined by a paltry apple theft,

He's but a bunch of bramble at the best,

Though proud enough to be the very bush

In which God's self was centred, and requires

Such cutting down, or trimming to the age,

As only such young men as I can give !

" God won't be wanted at the task."   You make

Good banter when you smiling answer thus.

But is there any reason in my words ?

Such reason, as at times you may have need of

In choosing flowers or ribbons at a shop,

Or making up your mind what place you go to

Just for that slip of time that lies between

The pleasant reach of quiet country life

And the long strain of London seasons? Think,

If I have haply uttered something strange,

There may be truth in strangeness, though the time

Likes best perhaps the well-worn counterfeits

That pass for verities, in the world you love—

But I have known, ere now, strange letters found

That had old love, as well as dust, upon them,

When making havoc, as they called my search,

In some long-cherished corner that I know.

If then I have too roughly handled truth,

In speaking of such things as are not wont

To make the staple of your morning talk,

You will forgive me. Pardon is a flower

That goes with grace in every royal crown ;

But queens may still be wearied—and I go,

For fear of tiring—it is getting late,

Good-morning, we may meet again, I hope."

LILY AND VIOLET.

A NATURAL SUGGESTION.

AS lily in the quiet eves,
    When woods are wet with dew ;
Ellen, thy holy beauty cleaves
    Me through and through.

I wait and worship as I pass,
    I cannot help but stay :
No saintly monk at early mass
    More prompt to pray.

As violet in the heated noon
    When all the air is faint ;
Alice, thy beauty breathes in June,
    No thought of saint.

I watch and wonder as I go,

    Yet cannot help but fly;

Some wicked spirit from below

    Lives in thine eye.

O lily in thy virgin cell,

    O violet in the sun,—

Why is it if I dream 'twere well

    Could both be one?

A PRAYER IN THE CITY.

LONDON, 1869.

AH, me ! the City groaneth at my feet,
 And all the crowd, oh God, is faint with woe;
Help have I none, nor any message meet.
 Teach me that I may know !

Behold the little children, everywhere,
 But not the little ones of old I knew;
Fledglings they seem, when all the woods are bare,
 Flowers, where there falls no dew.

Whose are they? for the parents heed them not,
 And men are all too busy as they pass;
Their place is with the shameless and the sot,
 Lost in the huddling mass.

The fair green fields, wherein the cowslips come,
    The streams whereby the tasselled grasses wave ;
These are as lands unknown ; the garret home
    Must hold them to the grave.

The song of birds, that in sweet seasons mate,
    And fill the pleasant May-time with delight,
Shall never reach these little slaves of fate
    Wrapped in their smoky night.

Yet have they guests that will not be denied
    As warders ever waiting at the door,
Grim Fever, with lank Famine at her side,
    These, and a thousand more.

See how the sunshine trembles on its way,
    So dark are all these alleys in the shade ;
Oh God, to think our palace builders stay,
    So near, yet undismayed !

We pile the marble for the rich man's tomb,
 We hang the satin at my lady's head ;
Why, then, are human lives within the gloom
 Less cared for than the dead ?

The babbling stream of fashion, comes and goes,
 And every bubble finds some fool to follow ;
But the great tide that heaves to speechless woes,
 Rolls on, and voices hollow,

Come from the hearts that should be first to bleed.
 "How very sad," they say, "that such things are ;
But 'tis the law of God, that one man's need
 Should light another's star."

Oh, idle prompting of the idle mind !
 That dares not pierce the veil that shrouds our lot ;
How shall the foolish swimmer hope to find
 Pearl, if he diveth not ?

From every side the voices call us now.

    " Come up and help, for we are well-nigh spent ;

The deeps are closing, and we know not how

    The succour shall be sent.

" We yet are brothers, though the primal stain

    Make labour seem a never-ending ill ;

And through the shadows, sorrow more than gain,

    Shall keep us brothers still.

" We ask for hearts tho' buried beating yet,

    We ask for hands, yet warm to bring us aid ;

These are the gifts that busy souls forget,

    These are the debts unpaid."

Surely our riches are not where we think,

    And the kind thought is more than all our store.

Give me the children's laugh ; the guinea's chink

    Is failing more and more.

Therefore, oh God, I tread this City street,

    With sadness that is not a foolish grief :

And from thine heavens I hear my message meet

    " Take heart—I bring relief."

MISCELLANEOUS SONNETS.

THOMAS HOOD.

A SONNET SUGGESTED BY A PERUSAL OF THE "HOOD MEMORIALS."

F ever to one hand full power were given
To sound at will the wayward chimes
of being,
With all our moods of mirth or grief agreeing,
This was the man ; yet with what sorrow riven,
As these fond records tell, his soul had striven,
While in thick mist of earthly doubts and fears
He wove for us, through long laborious years,
In fancy's rainbow woof all hues of heaven !
Yet nursed in gloom, with no proud flash of scorn,
Which while it lightens, blasts, his genius flew ;
But softly as the golden shaft of morn,
Whence all the wild wood laughs adrip with dew
So wit the bravest shot a kindly ray,
And fruitful wisdom filled his merriest lay.

A SONNET.

"IN MEMORIAM" DAVID GRAY, AUTHOR OF THE "LUGGIE"
AND OTHER POEMS.   DIED DEC. 3, 1861.

OH, rare young soul! Thou wast of such a
    mould

  As could not bear the poet's painful dower!

  Hence, in the sweet spring-tide of opening power,

Ere yet the gathering breeze of song had roll'd

Out on the world its music manifold,

  Death gently hushed the harp, lest storm or
    shower—

  Which surely life had brought some later hour—

Should snap the quivering strings or dim their gold;

Yet not the less shall tender memories dwell

  In those sweet notes—and sad as sweet they
    seem—

Which from the burning touch of boyhood fell;

  For long as little Luggie winds her stream,

And the twin Bothlin prattles down the dell,

  Thither shall many a pilgrim turn and dream!

A SONNET.

"IN MEMORIAM" JOHN CLARE, THE RURAL POET, WHO DIED
IN THE NORTHAMPTON COUNTY ASYLUM, MAY 20TH, 1864.

WHO hath not, when the summer woods were
    still,

Between the silver twilight and the dark,

Heard the stray note of throstle or of lark

Sound as a glad surprise o'er heath and hill?

Yet, ere the eager soul has ta'en its fill

Of the delicious music, jealous night

Has snatched the airy warbler from the sight,

And left us list'ning for the vanished trill.

So fell thy soft wood-ditties on our ear,

Sweet peasant poet, in a former day;

And all as swiftly fell the darkness drear

That quenched alike thy reason and thy lay.

But now thou wak'st to thine eternal morn,

May we not deem thy gentle notes re-born?

A SONNET.

ADDRESSED TO A YOUNG FRIEND, WITH A BOOK OF BALLADS.

SOME five years since I do remember well
    A little gold-haired lad, with looks of glee,
That many a winter-eve would mount my knee,
And in sweet lisp of childhood bid me tell
Wild tales, that seemed to work as with a spell,
So strangely did the poet's magic lays
That spake of Hiawatha's wondrous ways,
Haunt with weird power his Fancy's inmost cell;
And still I trust though summers onward roll,
And that young brain have busier thoughts in store,
Some stirring song as in those days of yore
May yet at times possess the eager soul.
Therefore this book of ballads would I send
To thee, dear Claude, that once did call me friend.

A SONNET.

WRITTEN IN A COPY OF WORDSWORTH'S POEMS PRESENTED
TO MY MOTHER ON LEAVING FOR THE LAKE DISTRICT.

THOU goest to the place where Wordsworth
    wrote,
Lived, loved, and died; his volume in thy hand
Thou hast the key to all the pleasant land
Of lake and stream, with valleys more remote
Than such as busy travellers care to note,
Coming and going in their ceaseless round;
For he in every common sight had found
Things deeper than are learned by idle rote
Of map or guide. The wisdom of the heart,
Born of the reverent love that beauty wakes
In the pure spirit; this it is that makes
The poet seem to some a man apart
From us and ours; but thou dost inly know
What all his musings mean and whence they flow.

IN MEMORIAM "SADIE."

SARAH WILLIAMS, AUTHORESS OF "TWILIGHT
HOURS."

OH sad sweet blossom, all untimely taken,
    Why did fair earth and fairer love of men
Dawn on thee if so soon to fade again ?
Yet such a sense of morning dost thou waken,
That earth and we are richer,—dews off-shaken
Before the sun is up, not less than when
All see them, feed the lilies of the glen ;
And thou hadst done thy task, though soon forsaken :
For thou wast but a snow-drop in the spring,
With all the weight of winter on thy bloom,
Yet through the yearning spirit couldst thou bring
Such thoughts of beauty from thine early tomb
As are not born in gardens passing fair,
Or longed-for summers that thou mightst not share.

THE RECOGNITION OF GENIUS.

A SONNET WRITTEN IN A POPULAR EDITION OF WORDS-
WORTH'S POEMS.

TIME was, Great Seer, when in thy mountain
place,
Thou sat'st apart, and river, lake, and glen
Had more to teach thee than the noise of men,
Or all the cares that stir our mortal race ;
Yet would the envious tribe, that springs apace,
In presence of all goodness, even then,
With busy havoc of the idle pen,
Have turned thy wise retirement to disgrace.
Now common as the all-encircling air,
And open as the waters or the wind,
We take thee, till the riches that we share
Seem as a part of being—undefined—
This is the fame true greatness only knows,
Pulse of the world's free heart, it comes and goes.

IN ROTTEN ROW.

FOUR P.M.

CHILD of my heart, I see thee in the crowd,
    'Mid all the fair sweet faces, fairest thou !
No touch of pride upon thy clear white brow,
Too pure in all thy beauty to be proud,
Thou sailest thro' my vision, like a cloud
That tak'st the dews, without the stains of earth,
And with the light of sunrise on its birth
Moves heavenward, leaving dead things in their
    shroud.
Yet are there thoughts I may not tell to thee,
And faces round about thou needs must know,
Not of God's heaven or earth as it should be,
But speaking Eden's bloom thro' Eden's woe.
God grant that thou may'st ever be pure and free
Even as the eternal fount whence all things flow.

ON WATERLOO BRIDGE.

ELEVEN P.M.

FOUL and forsaken, thrust from side to side,
    Poor child of sin, as things are counted sin,
What hope hast thou thus late to enter in ?
Scorned by the heirs of grace, the sons of pride,
Thou sittest staring blankly at the tide,
Away from home, unknown to kith and kin,
And think'st perhaps amid the waters' din
Thy shame, if not thy wretchedness, to hide—
Hope hast thou none, and through the blazing street
The stream of fashion flashes like a sword.
Is there no mercy ? Comes no message meet
For such as thee ? Off, Pharisaic horde !
Touch not a grief so holy—at His feet
She lies. " Go, sin no more !" exclaims her Lord.

A SONNET.

WRITTEN IN THE MEMOIRS OF ONE WHO WAS CALLED A
SCEPTIC.

" HE was a sceptic, and we need him not ;
The sunshine, and the calm that comes
with light,
Are better. We are happy, and the night
Was meant for sleep ; why should we idly blot
This fair life's page, with doubts beyond our lot ?
'Tis but the restless soul that scorns the right,
Shaping his own dim world, God out of sight—
And such was he—writing, he knew not what."
So gabble idle tongues of one that took
The burden of the mystery for his theme,
And held the souls' high prompting more than
book,
Or church, or creed : some think a prophet's dream
But foolish waste—yet in such moods are given,
Lights, that to waiting eyes are more than heaven.

RICHARD OASTLER.

BORN, 1789.—DIED, 1861.

OASTLER ! thy name is not among the great,
  As some count greatness; neither pen nor
  sword
Have brought thee glory; no man called thee lord,
With press of lackeys fawning at thy gate;
Nor thine the weary load that comes of state—
They better suit the vain and frivolous horde
That strike from day to day the passing chord;
Thine was a loftier dower—a nobler fate !
And tribute shall be paid in hearts, not gold,
And of such kind we pay thee of our best.
Let Cæsars take their homage as of old,
They have their pleasure; leave to God the rest.
Content thee, if through ages yet untold,
The little children rise and call thee blest.

A SONNET.

IN MEMORIAM : WALTER SAVAGE LANDOR, WRITER AND POET.
BORN, 1775.—DIED, 1864.

Suggested by Mr. John Forster's "Memoirs."

GONE with the frost of age upon thy brow,
　　But all the world's young beauty in thy song;
What balm hadst thou for those who suffered wrong,
What scorn for those who did it,—even now
Pulses of that high soul which could not bow,
Beat from thy foreign grave, till hearts that long
For times when only goodness shall be strong,
Yearn for the prophet's voice, to seal their vow.
" Ay, but his wreath was sullied," one will say,
" And shame was mingled with the old man's pride.
Strip off the laurels."   Oh, ungracious day !
That takes the long life toil, so fair and wide,
And with one cruel shadow mars it all.
Have *we* no dead leaves in our Coronal ?

GEORGE PEABODY,

MERCHANT AND HERO. A SONNET IN VIEW OF THE CITY
STATUE, UNCOVERED 23RD JULY, 1869.

REST, and the priceless blessing of the poor
    Be with thee, in the land that gave thee birth;
No better fruit grows on the teeming earth
Than such sweet thanks as spring beside the door,
Be it in populous town or lonesome moor,
That human kindness wings its healing flight,
And waking beauty in the homes of night,
Floods as with angel-track the humble floor;
Yet would we keep thine image near us still,
And, therefore, in the face of all our store,
We throne thee, and tho' fortune good or ill
Go with the restless tribes that round thee pour,
Long shall that kindly face true message bear,
And turn to mercy all our greedy care.

SONNET.

IN A FASHIONABLE CHURCH.—MAY, 1869.

THE air is faint, yet still the crowds press in :
    With stir of silks and under-flow of talk
That falls from lips of ladies as they walk,
Ere yet the dainty service doth begin ;
Ah me ! the very organ's glorious din
Is tuned to pliant trimness in its place ;
And over all a sweet melodious grace
Floats with the incense-stream good souls to win !
O God, that spak'st of old from Sinai's brow,
And Thou that laid'st the tempest with a word !
Is this Thy worship ?   Come amongst us now
With all Thy thunders if Thou wouldst be heard.
So tyrannous is this weight of pageantry,
Almost we cry, " Give back Gethsemane !"

VOICES OF THE 19th CENTURY.

NOT in one way do all Thy works go forth,
　　Great God that shap'st the course of things
　　　and men !
One with the plough, another with the pen,
Makes rich the glorious earth: from south to north,
And east to west, the seed of human worth
Falls in the furrows.　High on Sinai's top
Thy thunders roll, yet not less sweetly drop
The far faint notes that speak the linnet's birth.
Therefore I scorn not any human words,
Though lowly seem the lips from which they come :
All have some echo of the eternal chords
That reach from heaven to earth, and speak one
　　　home
We all are bound to.　In this book, our age
Takes up the endless tale—would 'twere a worthier
　　page.

HOMAGE AND HOMAGE.

LINES SUGGESTED BY THE ANNOUNCEMENT OF A LECTURE
ON "THE EXCELLENCY OF THE BIBLE," TO BE DELIVERED
BEFORE A YOUNG MEN'S CHRISTIAN ASSOCIATION.

SOME think the Bible poor, a pleasant fable,
    Fit for the peasant's soul, the scholar's table.
Others will have their talk about its wonders,
Blowing their penny pipes to Sinai's thunders.
Yet do I deem a reverent silence wholly
Dwells in the inmost shrine ; our human folly
At best but stains the whiteness that we touch,
And in God's presence prating over-much
Is but the noise of gnats that hum and flutter,
Marring the eternal psalm which He alone can
    utter.

THE TEACHING OF A YEAR.

VERSES IN MEMORY OF

A BELOVED BROTHER.

J. D. H. H. died 26th May, 1868.

THE TEACHING OF A YEAR.

VERSES IN MEMORY OF A BELOVED BROTHER.

M Y brother, now the year is round
  Since first I heard that thou wast
    gone,
Here in the silence have I found
  What means it thus to be alone.
We were not one in work or ways,
  We shaped through life no common plan ;
The rod and gun had most thy praise,
  With books and pen my fancies ran.
Yet seem there gaps where'er I go
  In paths whereon we seldom met,
Strange shadows passing to and fro,
  And shapes whereof the soul hath set.

Sometimes I wander in my dreams,
  Through haunts that are not traversed now ;
And music of familiar streams
  Flows past me, till the aching brow
Is fanned with breezes : whence they come,
  I know not, but some spirit says,
" Behold once more your boyhood's home,
  And drink the cup of other days."
The man of science shakes his head,—
  " A pretty problem, mark it well."
Some reflex force, I think he said,
  Within our brains is known to dwell.
And this it is that brings once more
  The buried days as once they were,
And mocks us with the ghostly store
  Of fancies lighter than the air.
Let be.   I ask not whence they are,
  To me they bring good tidings still :
And quiet as some guiding star
  They bear me onward at their will ;

And sometimes may I hear a voice,
 Though sounded low behind the veil.
It is thy own ; and I rejoice.
 Dear brother, other echoes fail,
But that which love and faith can call
 From spirits parted yet akin,
Sounds on for ever over all,
 And leads where other worlds begin.
The world, thou knowest, is not mine :
 Yet runs a chord from soul to soul,
And through the fleshly lattice shine
 The lights that show the common goal.
As prisoner parted by the bar
 From one that carries flowers of Spring :
So stand I listening from afar,
 Yet feel as if some angel wing
Swept by me in this earthly cell.
 While yet thy words are in mine ear,
I cannot bear to say farewell :
 I know that thou art ever near.

14

Therefore I weep not, though alone,
　　For I should wrong a noble name,
If breaking into idle moan,
　　I turned God's wisdom into blame ;
Grief is not worthy of its birth
　　If it be bowed to craven fears,
And eyes for ever turned to earth
　　Will lose the sunlight on their tears.
My grief is of a sterner kind,
　　And not the less I hold it true
If into sorrow's wreath I bind,
　　Fair hope to mingle with the rue ;
The day has still its task at hand,
　　And night has yet her dower of sleep :
Why should I mar my work, and stand
　　Aside from duty while I weep ?
Fear not that therefore love shall fail,
　　Or troth be faint as years go on ;
Surely the mast that stems the gale
　　Is seasoned when the storms are gone.

I know that thou art with me still,
  And love is surely more than death ;
Why murmur at the passing ill
  That simply takes the idle breath ?

I know that thou art more than I,
  And therefore with a holy awe
I bow my spirit, when or why
  Is measured by a higher law.

As yet we meet not face to face,
  But time shall be—I see the light,
And wait the message in my place,
  Dear brother, once again, good-night.

L'ENVOI

TO READER AND CRITIC.

FLOWERS for the hands of youth,
  Flowers for the crown of age :
Gathered on heights of truth,
  Gifts of the bard or sage.

Few have I such as these,
  Yet take, if you will, my store
Only some wild heartsease
  Plucked as I pass,—no more.

Yet as the years go by
  Turning the page to read,
Here, for some hands may lie
  Something more than a weed.

" Only some lines," you say,

"Written by one. Who knows

Whether he gather to-day

Cypress, laurel, or rose ?"

Matters it not; be earth's dower

Garden or grave-yard sod,

Only the soul's white flower

Blooms in the borders of God.

FINIS.